Pilot error: Summary

It is 1964, and Chris Nash is 20. His mc
whom Chris thinks is his father. He is th.......................
when she tells him that his real father was a pilot, John
Gregson, killed during the 2nd World War in an accident
training Australian air crews. Chris sets out to discover more
about the little-known incident. He tracks down his father's
only living relative, and visits the site of the crash, near a small
church in Bedfordshire.

In flashback we see what happened to Gregson during the
three days before the accident. He conducted his last
bombing flight over Germany, and was seduced by an actress
called Sarah. He visited his fiancée (Chris's mother), who
broke off their engagement; unknown to him she was pregnant
with Chris.

To commemorate the airmen who died in the crash, Chris
organises a memorial stone in the Bedfordshire churchyard,
and a church service. To his amazement a surprise guest
turns up: an Australian who was the one survivor.

In talking to local people who were involved in the accident,
and to his father's former engineer, Chris comes to believe
there were seven airmen on the plane, not six as previously
believed. And when he locates Sarah, the actress who
seduced his father 20 years earlier, she tells him something
that plays havoc with the lives of his whole family.

PILOT ERROR: A NOVEL

~ One ~

March 1964

Chris Nash finished his early shift in the Hammer and Pincers saloon bar just after one-thirty, and cycled home to Winchmore Hill. The streets of the nondescript North London suburb had been home for all of his twenty-one years, surroundings so familiar that he no longer noticed them: sedate, middle-class - frankly, dull. He free-wheeled up the drive of his parents' semi-detached house, left his bike against the garage door, and went into the kitchen to make himself a sandwich. His brother Gary was there, drinking yoghurt straight from the container. The radio was on full blast with the latest Rolling Stones single; Gary was a big fan.

'Do you want a spoon?' Chris said, at the cutlery drawer, seeing yoghurt roll down his brother's chin onto a new T-shirt.

'What would I want with a spoon?'

The response was characteristic: brief, unsmiling, slightly truculent. There was an unchanging sombreness about Gary, Chris thought; a face that seemed to be permanently in shadow. He was self-contained and gave no visible sign that life could be enjoyed rather than merely endured. Like Chris he was spare of frame and dark-haired, but there the resemblance ended. Despite the mere eighteen months age difference between them the pair had never managed to hit it off. Chris had no idea what was Gary was thinking at any given moment and he guessed the reverse was true. Nothing could be done about it. For the sake of peace in the family they managed an uneasy truce, though hostilities tended to break out once in a while.

'Guess what?' Chris said.

'What?'

'I'm getting a car.'

Gary switched off the radio. 'You can't even drive.'

'Oh no?' Chris imitated a racing car going through the gears. 'I've been taking some lessons. A friend's let me practise in his.'

'What sort of car?'

'It's an Austin 10.'

'Swish new model, then,' Gary said, heavy with sarcasm.

'It's a start. I got it for twenty pounds from a mate. A snip.'

'If it goes.' Gary's negative tone was remorseless. He leaned back against the sink, pondering other lines of belligerence. 'Have you got a licence?'

'Have to get one in a hurry. I've got the forms here. I need my birth certificate from Mum.'

Gary threw his empty yoghurt pot at the rubbish bin and left the kitchen without further comment. A 'good luck' or expression of pleasure would have been out of character. Chris had long since ceased to expect such civilities. Come to that, he had often been churlish himself where Gary was concerned. It was the way they were with each other.

When he'd finished his lunch Chris went upstairs. The house had four bedrooms, so he, Gary, and their sister Alison each had one to themselves while his father and mother shared the master bedroom. Given the smallish size of his own room Chris had to admit that the Liberator took up rather a lot of space, but he wouldn't have had it any other way. The model was on a small stand he'd constructed, and stood three feet across from wing tip to wing tip. It was the latest in a long line of model aircraft he'd put together: the most ambitious, and certainly the largest.

Why he always did bombers, rather than Spitfires or other glamorous fighters chosen by modellers of his generation, Chris would have found it hard to say with any conviction. Something about them appealed to him: their size, perhaps; the floods of fuel used to power the planes, or the massive cylinders of high explosives lurking in the bowels of the machines; the thought of long, monotonous journeys across Europe or the Atlantic Ocean, with men dotted about their lonely stations on the giant craft. He'd read a mountain of literature on the subject, imagined himself in the different roles of the bombers' crews. And why Liberators? Again the question generated no satisfactory answer in his mind. They seemed more elegant than the celebrated Lancasters, and he liked their role in coastal command. Whatever it was, Liberators had wormed their way into his affections and become something of an obsession.

He stood by the model for a while, running his hands over the fuselage. He reckoned the plane was about two-thirds finished, with all the main structural parts completed, built up from balsa wood during hour upon hour of detailed work. He had the weapons in place, and the ribbing on the wings, and had negotiated the tricky business of carving the propellers. The thought of putting in all the final details gave him one hell of a kick. Almost all of the cockpit had still to be done - the instrument panels, bulk-heads, and pilots' seat - and the navigator's table and bomb bay. Best of all he had the air-brushing of the aircraft's markings to come.

He put a Kinks record on his turntable and sat down at the work desk while Ray Davies's lyrics filled the room.

Eagerly pursuing all the latest fancy trends
'Cos he's a dedicated follower of fashion.

His modelling tools were always laid out ready for use: the knives and scalpels, tweezers, drills and files, the razor saw and steel rule. There were a couple of hours to spare and in that time Chris planned to put a coating onto the rear guns. They were already painted with a matt black and he now grated a 3B pencil against a sheet of glass-paper, scraped the dust together, and rubbed it with a forefinger into the barrel of the gun. The resulting sheen looked as near as dammit to real gunmetal. He was just about to seal it with a coat of varnish when the door opened, and his father came in.

On the rare occasions that Mr Nash came to Chris's room he could not resist a gesture in the Liberator's direction: a mixture of frustration and disdain, and another element that was harder for Chris to pin down. His father was a short, bullish figure of a man, with close-cut sandy hair and a noticeably florid face. In fact his features carried a permanent reddish tinge, like those of a man suffering from a high temperature. He was not aggressive, exactly, but possessed a somewhat volatile temperament. Chris found it all too easy to imagine him - a secondary school headmaster - lambasting a hall-full of unfortunate pupils. The scene had to be imagined, for it had been considered sensible for Chris and Gary to attend a different school, so neither of them had experienced their father's authority officially. At home he could be reasonable, even affectionate, but an eruption of temper was never far away - sometimes with Gary, and especially with Chris.

'Oh! Hello,' said Chris, as his father entered. Not very often you're home at this time of day.'

'I forgot something. I'm going back now.' Mr Nash hadn't taken his eyes off the Liberator. 'You're not still wasting your time on that thing, Chris?'

'It's two-thirds finished, I reckon.'

'That's not the point.' Tension was very apparent in the set of Mr Nash's neck and shoulders; there had been times when his whole body shook from suppressed irritation. 'How many hours has all that taken you?' he said.

'Heaven knows. A lot. It'd be like asking how many hours you've spent listening to Bach.'

The remark prompted Chris to jump up from his work desk and lift the needle off the turn-table. Musical taste was another difference between father and son. Mr Nash came forward a couple of paces and it was clear that he was trying to keep his voice calm. 'Can't you do something else with your time? This isn't going to help you develop, lad. You need something more - something to broaden you out. Everyone does.'

Chris sensed the affection behind the words, knew that his father wanted to help. But he knew too that there was an impulse to control, and resented it. The contrary interpretation won out, as it usually did. He shrugged.

'This is what I like to do.'

It was on the tip of his tongue to add a 'dad', but he didn't do it. When he was a kid his father had been 'daddy', but in the teen years he'd not made the transition to 'dad'. Something in their stop-go relationship had held him back.

Chris knew it was awkward, and felt sure his father was aware of it too.

Mr Nash made a gesture of resignation. 'Oh well...'

For his mother's sake, if not his own, Chris didn't want bad blood between them, so he tried to soften his stance on the Liberator business. 'Once I start college in September I'll have to cut down on this,' he said. 'I don't think the HND will be easy.'

Mr Nash grunted. Even this was a delicate area between them. He'd wanted his son to try for university when he left school three years earlier, but Chris had gone straight out to work for an insurance firm, insisting that he wasn't the academic type. Now he was about to start again, but an engineering qualification didn't meet Mr Nash's aspirations for him either.

'I came up to tell you,' his father said, changing the subject, 'There were two calls for you this morning after you'd left. One from that girl you know-'

'You mean Melanie?'

'Is that right?'

'You've met her. Is that who you mean?'

'That must be her.'

Mr Nash was never obtuse except on purpose. Melanie had been to the house a couple of times, but didn't make a habit of it. Chris could tell she hadn't really hit it off with his father. Come to that, he wasn't sure his mother had taken to her either.

'She asked you to ring back,' Mr Nash said. 'And your friend Sam phoned from the Hammer and Pincers. I wasn't sure who he wanted at first. He kept calling you "John".'

'Most of my mates at the pub do,' Chris said.

'Why, for God's sake?' His father turned full square on in the manner Chris knew so well, patience exhausted as yet another 'issue' transpired between them. 'Your name's Chris, isn't it?'

'Christopher John. You chose the names.'

Mr Nash seemed about to say something, then changed his mind. He was in a strange mood, febrile, almost tearful - Chris thought - if that were not such a ludicrous idea. 'You're Chris to me,' he said gruffly.

Chris had noticed the sensitivity about his name before, and couldn't understand the problem. Still aiming to appease, he tried to explain.

'They started calling me Christopher John - then it got shortened to John. I liked it.'

'So you encouraged it?'

Chris waved his hands helplessly. 'I suppose so, but...' He felt a little sorry for his father. So many things upset him. It was the battle of the generations magnified beyond all reason. 'Sam's been calling me "John" for quite a while now,' he said. 'You've heard him before.'

Mr Nash didn't answer but turned and walked out, breathing heavily. It was how many of their conversations ended.

Chris worked on the Liberator for the rest of the afternoon until he heard his mother come in around four, then went straight away downstairs.

He found her in the kitchen, beginning to prepare the evening meal. She was standing on tiptoe by the kitchen cabinets, reaching for the top shelf. Her Summer dress, drawn tight against the skin, emphasised his mother's slimness of figure. As always she proceeded with quick, light movements, more like a dancer than a housewife. The familiar actions gave the household much of its grace and charm. They were unselfconscious and instinctive. They seemed to say: I am ready to please; I have no special agenda of my own; I am open to you, whoever you are; I will do whatever would please you.

She turned to smile as he came through the door and he gave an answering grin. She smiled a lot. Neighbours would have said that she had 'a sunny disposition'. It was partly true, though Chris was aware of a darker side. Beyond the surface signs of good humour was a layer of melancholy; a sadness in the dark pupils of her eyes. She was cheerful but not carefree. He knew this to be so but had never enquired into the reasons. It was not the sort of thing sons did; you took your parents as they were. The formative years lay in the past.

'Any excitements in the Oxfam shop this afternoon?' Chris asked her.

'We had a man who'd brought in an old suit and left forty pounds in the pocket,' she said, moving deftly round the kitchen. 'Is that exciting enough for you?'

'Don't tell me you gave the cash back to him?'

She gave him a sideways look. 'I'm going to pretend you didn't say that.' She pushed her son against the wall during another circuit of the kitchen. 'I'll make a cup of tea if you'll sit down there out of the way.'

Chris did as he was told. He knew that she didn't mind his being there. Sharing his mother's company was as natural as breathing. He never needed to think about how to approach her, how to put matters to avoid upsetting her. Such things had always come naturally.

'What's for pudding? he said. It was an old joke between them.

'Pudding, he wants.' She put her hands on her hips. 'You youngsters don't know you've been born.'

'Oh no - here it comes.' He pretended to cower behind hands raised as a defensive shield. 'Don't tell me - the war years.'

'Yes, the war years,' she said. 'Not so long ago. No puddings then, my lad.'

'OK, OK,' he said. 'Listen Mum, good news. I'm buying a car. An old Austin 10.'

'Is that good news? Old cars go wrong, you know.'

'Ah, but if it does, you know I can fix it.' Chris's mechanical skills were legendary within the family.

She pretended to give him an appraising stare. 'I suppose so. Not sure I like the idea of you tearing about the roads in some old banger. What did you Dad say?'

'Er...I haven't told him yet.'

'Well tell him. Let him in on things.'

'All right,' Chris said. This too was familiar ground between them. 'The thing is - I need to get a licence in a hurry.'

She stopped what she was doing and looked at him uncertainly.

'So...could you find my birth certificate, please. I can't get one without it.'

He'd spoken casually, only half paying attention. Even so

he couldn't fail to notice the change in his mother's demeanour. Her swift movements round the room had stopped and she stood stock still, like someone struck by lightning. Her face had a hunted expression; her eyes were staring and transfixed.

Chris leaned forward in his chair, puzzled and slightly alarmed.

'Mum?'

Surely, he thought, she didn't really think he'd be in mortal danger on the roads. He was a sensible driver, pretty safe for his age group. What was the trouble, then? Had he not known better he'd have thought she was afraid of him.

'Give me the forms,' she stammered eventually. 'I'll send them off for you.' She made a show of going on with routines, but it was clear her mind wasn't on them. Her hands were actually shaking.

'Mum, I'm twenty-one. I reckon I can handle a post office form. Do you think I'm some kind of idiot?'

Normally she'd have said 'yes' to this, but today she simply shook her head. 'Of course not. It's just...'

He stood up and perched on the edge of the kitchen table, taking hold of both her arms. 'What is it? Are you OK? You look dreadful.'

She smiled, if it could be called that, and turned her head away. 'No, it's all right. I'll have to ask you father. I think he knows where it is.'

That was all Chris could get out of her. He went upstairs for a while, but when he came back to the kitchen half an hour later she was still there, sitting down, gazing at the surface of the table. There was no sign that she'd done anything at all in the previous hour. A peeled apple lay browning on the work surface.

When he looked back on that afternoon Chris was amazed that he hadn't fallen in sooner. There'd been at least one other occasion when he'd needed his birth certificate and his parents had sorted things out, but he'd thought they were being over-protective. There was no reason to think otherwise. You don't question something that has always been, since the first moments of consciousness. He could not know that his mother had endured twenty years of anxiety while the time bomb ticked away, awaiting some minor bureaucratic requirement that would set it off.

Mr Nash returned home at his usual time, around six. Chris was lying on his bed reading *Melody maker*, and heard his parents go to their bedroom, which was next to his. He thought nothing of it until their raised voices started to penetrate the adjoining wall. Although they were unaware of it he could occasionally hear some unwary, loud comment (usually in his father's powerful voice) during one of their arguments. This time he soon realised that a major row was under way. The heated exchanges bounced back and forth for some while. Unusually, his mother seemed to be holding her own. Once he heard her say 'sshhh', but the voices rose again regardless. Then the pair of them burst out of their bedroom into the passageway, and a few words reached him very clearly.

'I should be the one to do it, Susan,' his father's voice said.

'No, Reg,' said his mother, with a degree of force he rarely heard from her. '*I'll* tell him.'

By now Chris had begun to feel a certain apprehension about the sequence of events. He understood, if only dimly, that he was about to be told something that was causing his mother distress. His birth certificate was the catalyst, so in retrospect that 'something' seemed pretty obvious. But his defence mechanisms were working hard and when his mother came into the bedroom he was still unprepared.

She entered with a diffidence quite foreign to her usual manner. Her eyes were blotchy from crying. She held out a document, a cream, parchment-like paper with a criss-cross of red lines upon it.

'Here's your birth certificate,' she said, in a voice that was scarcely audible.

'Thanks Mum,' he said lightly, putting the paper down on the desk. 'Do tell me what's the matter.'

'Read it,' she said.

Still mystified, he took a look at the paper. The sparse, official details of a twenty-year old document stared out at him: Registration District of Edmonton; born third February, 1945;

name and maiden surname of mother, Susan Elizabeth Dilly. Only then did he become aware of a disparate element on the document: something his brain could not at first take hold of. Under 'name and surname of father' was written 'Edward John James Gregson'. He looked up at his mother and back at the document. 'Rank or profession of father: Flight Lieutenant, pilot, RAF, of 49 Gladwell Road, Finsbury Park N4'.

The words blurred on the page and re-formed into the same constellations. His eyes were negotiating the details in the usual way, but his brain appeared to be incapable of receiving their message. It was as if a short-circuit had occurred.

'What is this?' he said, pointing to the name that meant nothing.

Tears were coming from his mother's eyes in a continuous flow, like a small spring; they surged down her thin cheeks and dropped to the carpet. 'I'm sorry, dear,' she said.

'I don't understand.'

She began to speak but could not continue; sat on the bed, hands to her face. Her thin shoulders were shaking. Chris dropped to his knees and put his arms around her.

'Please stop, Mum. It's all right.'

At last she managed to stem the crying and regain some sort of control. Her face was wet and her dark eyes glittered, yet in a strange way she looked more animated than he had ever seen her.

'Reg isn't your father,' she said, speaking slowly and heavily. 'He's been a father to you and he's looked after you, but you're not his child. Your father is the man whose name is on the birth certificate.'

~ Two ~

The voice of Jack Vowles, the bomb aimer came very clearly over the aircraft's intercom. 'Left, skipper...left...left...'

In the pilot's seat Gregson edged the Lancaster left and awaited further instructions. It was the bomb aimer's moment: the one element of a flight when the pilot relinquished control to a member of his crew.

'OK skipper, hold it there...steady...'

Gregson checked on the instrument panel that they were coming in at 8,000 feet. Below the aircraft, Kiel glowed red. The docks were on fire, and most of the town too by the look of it. Several hundred bomb loads had preceded theirs.

'Steady, skipper...steady...'

Not for the first time the pilot noticed how they reverted to the formal 'skipper', rather than 'John', at moments of tension: take-offs, landings, bomb runs. This was the lethal part of every mission, when the huge aircraft held a steady course and presented a target. Flak came up in all the colours of the rainbow. Gregson knew his crew would be anxious, braced for the moment airmen dreaded: the impact of shells or cannon fire. He raised an eyebrow at Freddy Mitchell, the flight engineer in the adjoining seat, and made himself refrain from comment. No point throwing in a 'hurry it along, Jack'. The crew had their jobs to do, and a steady approach to the target was necessary. The bomb-aimer knew his work. Gregson did not envy him, stretched out below with only the thin metal skin of the fuselage and a perspex screen between himself and the unremitting flak.

'OK skipper, bombs away.'

The familiar mantra was an unnecessary one, because no pilot could fail to notice the effect as the 4,000-pounder left the bomb-bay; the aircraft leapt upwards, absurdly buoyant. Gregson always detected an ambivalence in himself at this moment. They had released their monstrous cargo, the weight of a London bus, to plunge onto the city below, but his interest was technical. He gave no thought to what happened when it hit the ground. Their job was to drop at a certain location, from a certain height; that was all.

That job was not over yet. The Lancaster carried incendiaries as well as the high explosive bomb, and they had to be released in a sequence over the next hundred yards. This demanded another ten seconds in a straight line, through flak which seemed heavier than ever. At its conclusion Gregson was about to weave so as to confuse the gunners below, when it happened. The blast was a new sound, different from all the others, and the impact that followed left little doubt that the plane had been hit. His stomach wallowed and he rushed to warn himself against panic. Think calmly. Don't get rattled. Where was the trouble? He began weaving anyway and craned his head in the cockpit looking for potential problems. No sign of damage or fire to the wings, or the precious fuel tanks. He got onto the intercom.

'Phil?'

'OK skipper.' This was the mid-upper gunner.

'Dave - you OK back there.'

'No problems, skipper.' The rear gunner's voice was steady. 'Are we hit?'

'Don't know yet. Albert - you OK?'

'I'm fine, John,' came the navigator's voice.

He was about to check the wireless operator when Freddy, beside him, exclaimed into the intercom.

'Christ almighty.'

Gregson saw immediately what had caused the engineer to cry out. Jack Vowles must have crawled up from the bomb aimer's compartment and staggered into the cockpit. He had arrived there in a reflex reaction, like a stroke victim who gets out of bed in the morning without knowing why. His oxygen mask was off and the skin of his face hung in shreds. Seeing Freddy's expression - somehow, through the carnage - Jack raised his hands to his face and brought them down swimming in blood. Only then did he realise the extent of the injuries. He reeled and half-fell to his knees.

Gregson forced himself to sound calm, knowing the crew

would react to his tone.

'Chris, are you there?' he called the wireless operator.

'Here, skipper.'

'Jack's got some face wounds - maybe worse. Get the rest-bed out. Come up into the cockpit and help him back onto it. Do what you can. Try and stop the bleeding.'

'OK skipper.'

'Albert - I need a course.'

'Right away, skipper.'

'Freddy.' The engineer was sitting right beside him, but against the noise of the engines it was useless to try and communicate except via the intercom. He pointed down the stairway to the bomb aimer's compartment. 'Get down there and see what the problem is.'

'Right away, skipper.'

The wireless operator appeared in the cockpit and half led, half carried Jack to the back of the aircraft, leaving a trail of blood behind him on the floor. Gregson took a fresh course from the navigator and waited for Freddy to return. His mouth was dry. Please let it not be bad news. The aircraft appeared to handle well enough. Flak continued to explode all around them in the lurid sky. The noise was unremitting.

Freddy clambered back up and attached his mouthpiece. 'Not too bad, John. Looks like we've had hot shrapnel ricocheting about down there. Still a lot of smoke around. Stinks of cordite.'

'Damage?'

'The steel rods holding the bomb sight have cut up - like so much firewood. The perspex is shattered. Must've been that which cut Jack's face up. Apart from that, we've been lucky. One problem though - the bomb doors are still open.'

'Thought so. I've tried closing them. No go. Thanks Freddy.'

He'd settle for that report of damage; even for Jack's face, if he were callously honest about it. The bomb-aimer must have pulled his head back after releasing the load, to allow for the sudden lift in the aircraft. It could have saved his life; his parents might get their son back alive, if disfigured, as long as nothing worse occurred. It was bad luck, though. Normally air crews welcomed flak, which was infinitely preferable to an attack from fighters.

'John, it's Chris here.'

'Go ahead.'

'These cuts are awful...it's a real mess, skipper..' The wireless operator's voice trembled on the edge of panic.

'All right, Chris...steady now.'

'It's only his face, though. At least I think so. I've got him under sedation.'

'Good. Keep him comfortable, if you can. And thanks for handling that.' He made his voice sound a bit more formal. It was a trick of his to try and atone for his youth; sometimes he wondered why the men followed him at all. 'OK, all crew. You heard that. The plane's all right - except the bomb doors are stuck open. We're going straight back home. You're to keep an eye open for those fighters - especially near the Dutch coast. They'll be about. Meanwhile let's keep it quiet, unless something else happens.'

In the cockpit he settled back to his main business of flying the plane. The strong head wind restricted the aircraft to a speed of 85 knots. The roar of the engines dominated everything, along with the smell of fuel, rubber and dope. His shoulders ached. He was cold. Down on the ground it was mid-July, but at 20,000 feet summer signified very little. His armpits sweated under the layers of pullover and jacket but his feet were freezing. He fingered Susan's nylon stocking round his neck and for a moment recalled the sensation of her thigh against his palm, but the image soon drifted away. Most of the boys said they could not think about women in the air. Doing his job in the aircraft above the clouds was as much as a pilot could manage. The mere handling of the brute Lancaster took all Gregson's strength. He was dirty and tired; tired with the deep, pervading exhaustion that came from worry and the gauntlet of risk endured through the long nights of mission piled on mission.

He longed for cloud but the moon showed up the grey landscape below them. They crossed the Kiel canal and then the Frisian Islands came into view: the chain of elongated land-forms that some benign deity had scattered along the

Dutch coast for the benefit of British airmen returning home. Despite everything - the noise, the violence, the unremitting danger - Gregson still enjoyed handling the aircraft high above Europe and guiding it back to touch down in the heart of the British countryside. He knew that most pilots did. It was why they had applied for their suicidal jobs in the first place. The cockpit, with its perspex surrounds, had a light, airy feel far removed from the unlovely body of the fuselage and all the paraphernalia of wires and rods that adorned the crude metal skin. Positioned above the main body of the plane he felt detached, almost God-like. His view of sea and sky stretched through 180 degrees. If there was an up-side to the absence of cloud it was this corny vista of rippling water in the moonlight. Better to die with a good view, the crews would say in their more mordant moments.

It was curious how men could feel lonely in a crew of seven but they were all isolated by the layout of the plane and the roar of its engines. He was luckier than most because of the proximity of the flight engineer. He liked having Freddy beside him, even though they could scarcely communicate. Gregson knew pilots who disliked their flight engineers and it rendered missions that much bleaker. He glanced across now and got back a characteristically quizzical expression. The luxuriant moustache sprouted visibly behind the oxygen mask. There was reassurance even in the set of Freddy's shoulders, the bulky, comfortable figure. From the moment they'd met, two years earlier, they had hit it off, with nothing much in common beyond a passion for aeroplanes and flying.

If he felt lonely in the pilot's seat, how would his rear gunner be feeling? Gregson spoke almost guiltily into the intercom.

'Dave. How are you feeling back there?'

'OK skipper. I'll be putting in for some new feet though, when we get back.'

'I know. You should have been a wireless operator.' The man on the transmitter was always the warmest member of the crew. 'Chris, will you come in. Tell me about Jack.'

'He's quiet, John. Sedated. I think he'll -'

'Corkscrew, port - go!'

The rear gunner's voice exploded back again with an

urgency which could not be contradicted. Gregson heard the rear turret machine guns open up and threw the control column forward, full port rudder, causing the aircraft to dive to port. It was too late. He heard a frightening crash as the Lancaster was hit and felt a corresponding loss of control in the dive. For a long moment he fought to regain mastery. The odour of vomit - Freddy's invariable reaction to turbulence - came into the cockpit but the engineer's voice still came steadily over the intercom, relaying the comment every airman dreaded.

'Starboard outer on fire.'

Instinct took over from any kind of rational thought as the pilot struggled with the Lancaster. For a couple of minutes it was touch and go. He pulled her out of the dive and feathered the damaged engine. Freddy shut off the fuel cock. Gregson felt a relief that bordered on exhilaration when his engineer's voice came on again.

'Fire's out, skipper.'

Gregson drew a deep breath. 'What else?'

'Problem with the starboard inner, too. White smoke. Must be losing coolant. No better than half power, I'd say.'

'Dave.' Gregson called the rear gunner. 'Have we lost that fighter?'

'Can't see him, skipper. Sorry about that. Came from nowhere.'

'It's not your fault, Dave. Are you OK?'

'Think so, skipper.' Just a slight hesitation. 'Don't worry. Get us home.'

There was no need to tell Freddy to check on the damage. He was already pulling switches and levers, checking distances with the navigator in the rapid, methodical way that made him such a valued companion. Gregson busied himself with the task of flying the aircraft on two good engines, and those two on the same wing. Full right rudder just about did it, if he held the port wing down. They were at 7,000 feet but losing height. The fuel position would be crucial. At the back of his mind he couldn't keep out a passing reflection on their change of luck. They had been so fortunate on recent trips, coming through them with minimum damage to aircraft and personnel. Now they faced the same sort of desperate situation that so many had encountered before them; and a good number of those had not lived to tell the tale.

'The hydraulics are knocked out,' Freddy came back on. 'And no wireless. We're going to have fun landing.'

'Fuel?' Gregson's voice was urgent.

'Albert reckons we've twenty minutes to spare and I agree, more or less. There's a big hole in the starboard wing and a lot of smaller holes in the fuselage. What with that and the bomb doors open we're bloody unstable. Makes things very heavy on fuel. Could get worse. Height will be the problem'

'Ditch everything that moves. Everything. Chris, would you organise that, with Albert.'

'Righto, John.'

'Just keep me up to speed on the fuel situation.'

After the brief moments of wild, cathartic activity, now began the long haul back to the British coast. Bombing raids were like that. Crews were on their own in a solitary battle to survive, and no-one else could help. The pilot bore the brunt of responsibility, mentally and physically. Gregson was slight in build and the sheer effort of handling the Lancaster for eight unbroken hours took a toll. To maintain the aircraft more or less level he had to keep the right rudder permanently down, and the muscles in his right leg ached horribly; he found some relief by bringing both feet into the holding position. With all the damage they had sustained the Lanc felt like a different plane; it fought against him, baulked his intentions. Despite all his efforts they lost height steadily across the North Sea. He prayed that there were no fighters about. Unable to duck and dive, with their gun turrets out of action, they would be the simplest of targets for any German sharp-shooters.

Beside him Freddy juggled fuel between the four tanks, trying to eke out every last drop to get them across the English coast. Meanwhile the crew were jettisoning all the equipment they could lay their hands on: guns and ammunition, smoke bombs, the navigator's Gee set, armour plate. The Elsan toilet plunged down after them, followed by all the usual, hoary old jokes. When all this was done Gregson checked the crew again, and got replies from everyone.

Briefly, he allowed himself to dwell again upon their bad luck. You expected to die during a tour of thirty trips; at least he did, and he knew many airmen felt the same. Optimism was rare, an almost misguided luxury. All the same on their last trip, with a relatively trouble-free tour in the bag, they deserved better. Within a few days Gregson would have been put down for the easy option of training duties, and his crew to equally safe activities.

He had felt a tremor of unease when this Kiel mission was announced - the first major attack on a German city for months. Recent weeks had seen the squadron suffer only minor losses as they took on a series of short-range targets: railway yards and flying bomb sites in France, naval vessels in Boulogne harbour, support attacks in the Normandy battle area. All new manoeuvres in a rapidly changing war. Now this: on their last trip - their very last trip - back to the old style, long-range attack with its high quotient of 'missing' British planes. And short odds now on their adding to those statistics.

Gregson did another check on the crew. From the navigation area Albert reported that Jack was still quiet, under sedation. When the pilot called Dave, in the rear gun turret, he was met with silence.

'Dave - are you OK?' he insisted

After another pause, the voice came faintly. 'Yes - OK.'

'Stay awake, Dave.'

'Sorry, skipper.'

Something in his voice made Gregson enquire again. 'Dave - are you sure you're OK?'

'I'll be fine, skipper. Just get us there and don't worry about me.'

The pilot had to let it go; he had other things to think about. They were down to a thousand feet as the Lancaster crossed the English coast, somewhere between Cromer and Lowestoft. It was an immense relief to see dry land below them, and English land at that, but he knew the real danger began now. In confirmation Freddy's voice came over the intercom.

'John - we need to decide. There's less fuel than I thought. We'll never make Mepal, of course. Not enough to divert to Woodbridge, either.'

'I can't stay up much longer. And I can't circle round, either. We need to hit a field first time.'

'I know.'

His navigator broke in. 'It has to be Coltishall, skipper. It's the first one we go near on our present course.'

'That's not a bomber site, is it?'

''Fraid not. Spitfires.'

'Can't be helped. Let's do it. We'll take some fences with us if need be. I want the whole crew back behind the central spar. You too, Freddy.'

'You'll need help up here, skipper. We've got to get the wheels down.'

'Freddy, behave yourself -'

'It's no use, skipper. I've got my job to do.'

Freddy was usually a stickler for following orders, not least because of their close friendship, and Gregson took his mini-rebellion as an omen: that the engineer expected the worst. The pilot was filled with foreboding as Albert guided him in. Without the wireless he could not talk to the people at Coltishall and he simply flashed his landing lights and hoped the runways were clear. They would not be too pleased to see a Lancaster crashing down on a strip designed for fighters.

In a situation like theirs the pilot had to manage an awkward balancing act psychologically: to make his crew aware of the risks but at the same time avoid mawkish prognosis. They would all be well aware anyway that their chances were less than 50/50. At least there was hardly any fuel left in the tanks, which reduced the ever-present danger of fire.

'All crew,' he said, as calmly as he could manage. 'You know the emergency landing positions. Once we're down you're to get out of the craft as quickly as possible. Chris, Albert - you get Jack out. And good luck everyone.' He wanted to say how much he'd enjoyed flying with them but this might have struck an elegiac tone that would have been quite wrong for the circumstances.

'Thanks, skipper. Good luck to you.' This was Chris, and his voice was echoed by others.

He envisaged them sitting with their backs against the main spar which ran across the fuselage, hands behind their heads.

Beside him Freddy was operating the emergency system that enabled the undercarriage to be lowered automatically.

'Undercarriage down, skipper. Now let's see if it holds.'

They passed over the base perimeter lights at twenty feet. The runway looked absurdly short after those they were used to. He came down quickly, watching the ground rise to meet them and the runway lights racing past. As the wheels hit the ground the Lancaster's undercarriage collapsed, the mechanism obviously shot through. Gregson switched off the engines and reflected, with characteristic fatalism, that the lack of brakes was irrelevant now. The ground raced past as they slid on and on upon the belly of the plane, churning up the airfield till they passed the end of the runway. Gregson heard a tearing sound as the plane took away a fence and barbed wire, and still they careered on. We're sliding all the way back to Cambridgeshire, he thought. At last they came to rest, in an eerie silence. There was no sign of fire. We're alive, was his first reaction.

Freddy took off his mask. 'Your best landing yet.'

They got out quickly through the top hatch and climbed down to help the others. It was peaceful in the darkness, in this alien field. Trees fringed the perimeter and some cows, greyly visible in the mid-distance, were ambling forward in muted curiosity. There was no sign of movement from the direction of the base. Chris and Albert had got the rest bed well clear of the aircraft and were laying it down on the turf. They were careful but Jack's figure still stirred uneasily. Gregson flinched at the sight of his face, even in the darkness.

Chris took Gregson's arm. 'Thanks, skipper. We're alive.'

'Well done, skipper,' said Albert. 'Bloody good show.'

Gregson was touched by the comments, unusually serious for airmen, but then looked around in alarm.

'Where's Dave? Has anyone seen him?'

'He's not come out yet,' said Chris.

Gregson moved towards the side hatch, suddenly apprehensive. Freddy grabbed at his arm.

'Best to wait, John, till the fire vehicle gets here.'

'We'll wait for ever at this base,' said Gregson, ducking into the hatch. 'You're all to stay here.'

He moved as quickly as he could to the rear of the Lancaster, scrambling over the spar of the tail until the closed armoured doors came into view. Not for the first time he recoiled from the idea of spending eight hours on the trot in the rear-gunner's freezing environment, with inadequate fire-power and very little armour protection. It was the one job in the aircraft he couldn't bring himself to do. Dreading what he might find, he wrenched open the doors. Dave was lying face forward with his head cradled on his forearms.

'Dave. Dave.'

Gregson reached forward and felt the gunner's pulse, as they had been trained to do. No response. He turned the man over, struggling in the cramped conditions, opened Dave's flying jacket and saw the traces of blood on his clothes: stains that he had not wanted to see, in places where he had not wanted to find them. He envisaged the letter that must now be written to the gunner's parents; saw the telegram being delivered, and the expression on the face of the gunner's mother as she opened her front door to the messenger boy.

The pilot clambered out to rejoin the others; they stood in a semi-circle puffing cigarettes, still waiting for help from the base. Albert was relieving himself against the tail-plane. His piss splattered into the grass, the only sound in the meadow.

'Dave's dead,' Gregson said.

They stared at him. 'He didn't say a word -' Freddy began.

'No. The signs were there, though. I should have spotted them.'

'And if you had, John.' Freddy took his arm. 'Would it have made a difference?'

'Probably not. He knew he'd bought it.' Gregson was a hundred years away from tears but he felt and almost tasted a wave of despair. 'He decided not to bother us - to go quietly.'

'He was always an independent bugger,' said Chris.

As he spoke they saw headlights approaching across the airfield, and the station commander's car raced through the gap in the fence and drew up beside them. A furious group captain jumped out. He stared pointedly as Albert finished relieving himself and began buttoning up his flies.

'Who's in charge here?'

'I am,' said Gregson, still with his back to the newcomer. 'Flight Lieutenant Gregson.'

'What the hell do you mean by this, churning up my airfield.' The man was beside himself with rage. 'Can't you people learn how to fly. You've not even had permission to land yet.'

The pilot turned to face the newcomer, feeling an immense weariness. The man's accent had already gone a long way to explain his attitude. Class tensions in the RAF were common enough. The force needed volunteers for their death-runs into Germany, and working-class boys had supplemented traditional entrants from the public schools. Gregson had rarely been bothered by their differences but at this moment he had no emotional energy left for restraint. The group captain was the worst kind of public school product and with the unfailing instinct of his class the man had already placed Gregson, from his one brief comment, in a different category. They might have been in a different war.

The pilot took several paces towards the group captain. 'You don't seem to have noticed that we've been shot up. I have a man badly injured here,' he said, pointing to Jack's form on the ground. He spoke in a voice that was almost menacingly quiet. 'I've a dead comrade in the aircraft. I want an ambulance on the scene, and I want it quickly. There's a risk of fire - and still no sign of your fire vehicle ten minutes after landing. So why don't you button up your opinions and start doing your job.'

If Gregson's crew were startled by this outburst from their habitually courteous and understated skipper, the group captain was rendered speechless. When he did manage to get some words out they were almost a splutter.

'You keep that up and you'll find yourself on a court-martial, my lad.'

'We'll see.' The pilot kept his voice low but he seemed to be shouting from the tree tops. He stepped forward again until his face was inches from the officer's. 'Meanwhile you'll get those facilities over here now, or I'll hit your fucking supercilious face so hard you'll look like my bomb-aimer.'

Freddy gazed at his skipper, astonished. In two years of

flying he had never heard Gregson use the obscenity before - uniquely, amongst his RAF colleagues.

The pilot's outburst had an immediate effect nevertheless, and procedures at the base swung belatedly into action. The fire-people turned up and did their work. A doctor arrived to take charge of Jack Vowles and got him into a hospital; they predicted he would survive, albeit badly disfigured. An ambulance removed the body of the rear-gunner and the rest of the crew took transport to the debriefing room. The base was enjoying a quiet night and Gregson's men were dealt with quickly; the interview was more than usually futile and they got no information about the success, or otherwise, of the raid on Kiel.

Afterwards they went into the mess and sat together eating their bacon and eggs, not talking. Arriving at a different base amongst unfamiliar faces was always unsatisfactory. Airmen craved routines. Any exhilaration they might have felt from completing their last tour trip was dissipated by Dave's death and the accident to Jack; by an unfortunate chance there was an empty chair at the table and the absence of their comrades was palpable.

Before they ate Gregson had visited the control tower to report to the Mepal base and request transport back. Waiting for it seemed to go on for ever; they sat silently in mess armchairs, absorbed in their own thoughts, falling asleep one after the other. At last an orderly shook Gregson awake and told him that an 8-cwt van had arrived from Mepal to take them back.

The crew barely seemed to be conscious during their transfer to the van, but Freddy was reasonably alert and sat down beside Gregson at the front. Before the journey started the WAAF driver handed Gregson two envelopes, which she said his orderly had urged her to take along.

The pilot opened the first, read it with difficulty in the semi-darkness of the vehicle, and made an involuntary exclamation.

'Bad news?' Freddy asked.

'In a way. They're my orders for what happens next. Training duties, as expected. Aussie crews.'

'Could be worse. When do you start?'

'That's the bad news. Two days time.'

Freddy sighed. 'Work horses - we're nothing more.'

'Ever flown from Bassingbourn?' the pilot asked. 'That's where I'll be.'

'Never have. Cambridgeshire again.' Freddy turned towards him. 'Does it say whether I'll be with you?'

'Reading between the lines, I'm afraid you won't. They've obviously got other plans for you and the crew.'

Freddy grunted, and they sat in silence for several miles.

'I'm really sorry about that,' Gregson said eventually. 'I'm going to miss you a lot.'

'Likewise,' Freddy said. 'We'll keep in touch though.'

More miles passed, and they said nothing. The WAAF was a good driver, keeping the van moving but taking care in the blackout. Not surprisingly they met almost nothing else on the roads at this time in the early morning. She was a pretty girl, Gregson thought, taking a sideways glance at her in the front seat, and she knew better than to try and chatter to airmen back from a mission.

He remembered the other envelope. It looked like a personal communication and the handwriting on the outside was unfamiliar. He tore it open and, reading the contents, exclaimed again.

Dear John

Remember me! You visited my dressing room a few days ago after seeing my

play at the Lyceum. I enjoyed talking to you, and wondered whether we could

meet again. I understand from your orderly that you are likely to have a few days

free and thought we might meet up tomorrow (Tuesday) - maybe go for a meal

in town? If not tomorrow, some other time. Can you telephone to let me know

one way or the other? I do hope you can make it. I'd like to see you.

Yours

Sarah Frielen

Reading it, Gregson found the blood rushing to his head, and was glad they were sitting in darkness. He saw Freddy gazing enquiringly at him and tried to collect his thoughts.

'It's from Sarah,' he blurted out.

'Sarah?'

'That actress...remember? We went to see her after the play.'

'Oh! Sarah.'

They had been to see the Terence Rattigan play *Flarepath*, about the wives of a bomber crew. It was only the second time in his life that Gregson had visited a theatre. Both he and Freddy had been struck by her performance and after the play they decided - it was the sort of thing airmen did - to try and meet the actress in her dressing room. Because of the bombing theme, and because they were in uniform, and because it was the war, they had been allowed in. She had sat in a dressing gown wiping make-up from her face, talking to them for quite a while. Gregson remembered now that she had written down their names and squadron. It was one of those spur-of-the-minute things and he'd thought no more about her. In fact at the time he reckoned she had taken a fancy to Freddy; and that Freddy had been distinctly interested in her.

'She wants to see me,' he said, sensing a slight awkwardness between them, perhaps because of this.

'*Oho*! And are you going?'

'I don't know,' Gregson said, untruthfully, for he had already decided to ring her and accept.

An army truck loomed out of the darkness and went by uncomfortably close, shaking the van on the camber. Because of the black-out it only became visible at the last moment.

'What about Susan?' came Freddy's voice, echoing a thought that was already worming away inside Gregson's conscience.

The last thing Gregson wanted was to talk about Susan, but he couldn't bring himself to clam up with Freddy.

'Now you mustn't be jealous, Freddy - just because you

fancy Sarah yourself.' He tapped his friend on the shoulder. 'It's no big deal, you know. She's suggesting a meal together - not a night in a four-poster.'

'Hmm. You young chaps!' The WAAF girl was looking stolidly up the road ahead and Freddy gave a tiny nod in her direction to indicate that the subject matter needed to be shielded from station gossip. 'I sometimes feel like a grandfather in this unit.'

Gregson threw him a look which said 'here we go again'. It was true all the same that the men looked up to Freddy. He was twenty-six - a mere five or six years older than most of them - but that seemed to cover a lifetime's gulf in experience. Freddy was a man, not a boy. It was there in the expressive details of his face. The florid moustache was merely a comical add-on, like a clown's red nose, an RAF symbol.

'Think of the chaps in our squadron,' Freddy went on, 'I reckon most of them know nothing about women at all. They bang on about them all the time, they chase them around every bar in the county, there are pictures of half-naked film stars everywhere - but that's all that happens. They don't understand anything about the buggers - and that's dangerous, believe me.'

Gregson wished Freddy would shut up. The comments were carefully framed as generalisations but he knew they were directed at him; what was worse, they were too close for comfort.

Freddy turned in his seat to look directly into the pilot's eyes. 'Think it through,' he said softly, so that his voice was inaudible to the WAAF driver above the noise of the van. 'Don't forget, I saw you with Susan when she spent that weekend up here. I saw how you were together. I tell you, I envied you, John.'

' I know, Freddy, believe me. I'm going to see Susan on Tuesday. Nothing's changed. Don't make a mountain out of a mole-hill.'

'Sure, sure - but please be careful. Sarah's different from the sort of girls we know. She's an actress. They've cut themselves loose. They're outside the usual social structure. Can have an unpredictable effect...apple-carts upset, and all that...know what I mean?'

'All right. All right.'

'And anyway, you poor devil, you know she really fancies me.'

The return to jokey RAF banter signified that Freddy's lecture was at an end, and no more was said until the van pulled in at the base. They woke the rest of the crew, thanked the WAAF driver, and walked to their quarters laden down with flying gear. Dawn was coming up over the airfield, framing the stark outlines of Nissen huts against an enormous sky. Gregson and Freddy led the way.

'And since you are going to see Sarah later today,' Freddy said boldly, 'Would you like me to look in on that hound of yours?'

Gregson looked grateful. 'Bitsa would be delighted, of course. I think she's fonder of you than me.'

'It's the way I fondle her ears. I find it has the same effect upon women.' Freddy guffawed. 'Tell you what. Are you sure you're going into London to see Susan tomorrow?'

'Of course I am.'

'Then why don't I take Bitsa into mine this evening, and you can pick her up tomorrow night. You'll be coming to the booze-up in the evening?'

'Not sure what time I get back from Susan, but I'll look in at least.'

'"Look in" isn't good enough. You have to *be* there, John.' Freddy was unusually insistent. 'Chance to say goodbye, you bugger.'

They said muted farewells to the rest of the crew and dispersed separately to their huts. Gregson was desperate to put his head down on a pillow, but something made him stand and watch Freddy's solid frame until it disappeared into an adjoining hut. The sudden rush of sentiment was unusual. Comings and goings were standard procedure for airmen. Friends and acquaintances had exited from Gregson's life with no more fuss than a chalked aircraft number rubbed from the daily flight board. It was only now, as the moment of separation was upon them, that realisation came through to him: saying goodbye to Freddy would mean a lot more than that. In two turbulent years Freddy's friendship had provided the emotional ballast that he badly needed. He was going to miss him a lot. Already he felt more exposed, more vulnerable, as if a layer of self-confidence was peeling away.

The pilot turned and pushed his way into his own hut. He flung his equipment onto the floor, threw himself down on the bed and fell asleep instantly.

~ Three ~

March 1964

A hundred things fell into place for Chris as his mother said the words 'Reg is not your father'. He felt as if he'd been looking into a kaleidoscope with a picture that was muddy and confused, had shifted the base and brought his whole life into focus, brighter than before with every individual piece matching its neighbour. He waited for her to go on.

'I should have told you this years ago,' she said. 'Of course I should. You have no idea how hard it is to find the right time. I let it go, and let it go...'

'It's all right. You've told me now.'

She blew furiously into a handkerchief, but her eyes were still streaming. 'I haven't cried like this in years,' she said, with a little laugh. 'There are so many things I have to tell you.'

Chris had one thought in his mind. 'Tell me about my father.'

'Yes, of course.' She composed herself and he felt like a child again, sitting at his mother's knee to hear a story. 'He was a pilot - a very good one, I was told. He had a way with engines and machines, just like you. You can't imagine how strange it's been, Chris, seeing you so caught up with the war and aircraft, and all that...like something inherited. I know Reg has hated it.'

'It must have been odd.' Chris wanted to keep Reg out of it; Reg, not his father any more. 'Edward,' he said, changing the subject and testing the sound of his father's name. Edward.'

'Not really,' she said. 'That's another strange thing. You know how some of your friends use your second name. It was the same with your father. His parents called him Edward, but to all his friends he was John - his second name. He was always John to me.'

'Where did he live?' Chris said, jumping ahead again. There were a dozen questions he wanted to ask all at once.

'He was brought up in Finsbury Park, a few miles from our house in Edmonton. We met in church.' She grinned wanly. 'Not a place anyone's likely to find you, my lad. He was visiting an aunt who lived in Edmonton. I got talking to her after the service, and she introduced me. Once we'd met...well, we liked each other straight away.'

Chris could see the affection in her eyes even now, decades later. In all probability she'd not talked about the man for the past twenty years. How often had she thought about him? Strange landscapes threatened to roll into view: all sorts of things he didn't know, about his own mother.

'We got together when we could,' she continued. 'You have to remember there was the war going on. Everything was so difficult. He was on bombers through most of it - in the air more often than not. They led an awful life. When he could, he came down to see me in Edmonton.' She broke off and gave another strange laugh through her tears. 'This is so difficult, Chris. You can't imagine.'

He put a hand over hers. One question was burning his tongue, but he couldn't bring himself to ask it.

'The day you were started,' she said, using her generation's euphemism for conception, 'We went to Epping Forest. It was where people from Edmonton went for an afternoon out. You took a bus down past the River Lea. May, it was - the thirteenth of May. A lovely day.' He saw his mother's expression change as her thoughts went back over the years. 'We had some lunch at the Royal Forest Hotel and walked down to the edge of the wood. It was there...' She shot a quick glance at him, embarrassed. 'You have to realise, Chris, how different thing are now between youngsters. We didn't have the pill, or anything like that. I expect you and Melanie...'

Chris had never discussed with her - or his father - what he and Melanie got up to, and didn't want to start. 'Go on, Mum,' he said.

'We were so ignorant in those days,' she said. 'I can hardly credit it now. Young people had no experience. We were going to get engaged, John and I. We were committed to each other. He wanted to do it, and...well, so did I, to tell you the truth. It did happen in wartime, more than people would admit. I trusted him...' She fell silent, and he knew that a painful memory had come back to her; something she had not revealed.

'And you got pregnant?' he said.

'Yes.' She smiled, and shook her head slowly from side to side. 'Our only time, and...'

He had to ask the question that was hammering away, though he was sure he knew the answer. 'Mum - is he alive? Is my father still alive?'

She reached out and put a hand on his arm, and for him the gesture took an eternity. 'I'm sorry, Chris. He was killed. I'm really sorry.' Her eyes overflowed again.

They stayed like that for quite a while, with Susan on the edge of the bed and Chris on the floor beside her. His room was like a time capsule from which all other existence had been obliterated. She cried for something that had happened twenty years earlier, and it was as though she was giving proper vent to her feelings for the first time. As he comforted her Chris tried to get a hold on his new identity. In the space of ten minutes he'd lost the father he thought he had, found another, then lost him too. He couldn't shed tears for John Gregson; it was just a name, a symbol for someone he had never known. Sympathy were reserved for his mother. But already he felt the first stirrings of curiosity: the need to find out more about this man, and by doing so more about himself.

He got to his feet and paused by the Liberator model, running a forefinger along the fuselage.

'No, it wasn't a Liberator,' she said, in response to his look. 'He was killed in a Lancaster.'

'Go on, Mum. Tell me about it, please.'

'Yes, I suppose you need to know.' His mother was on her feet too, smoothing down her dress, then sitting on the chair at his work desk. She was beginning to get herself together again. 'The last time I saw John I'd just discovered I was pregnant. He came down to Edmonton to see me straight after the end of his bombing tour and...it all went horribly wrong. I was in a funny mood. I didn't tell him. I didn't want him to marry me just because I was pregnant and...oh, the war and everything...it was silly.'

He knew immediately that she was holding something back. He could sometimes read her mind in this way, and she his. 'What do you mean, Mum - "and everything"?'

She looked up ruefully. 'All right, there was something else. A right little clever clogs, aren't you, spotting that.'

'Only twenty years late.'

'I didn't really want to tell you this-'

'Please tell me everything. I need to know.'

'Do you?' She looked uncertain, but went on with it. 'That last day I found out that he'd seen someone else. I don't know who she was, but her name was Sarah. It doesn't matter how I know.' She saw his face and said quickly: 'Don't hold that against him, Chris. It was a passing affair, I'm sure.'

He felt immediately outraged. 'How could anyone not prefer you?'

'Thank you, my loyal son.' She bowed her head in mock gratitude. 'Don't blame him. These things happened all the time in the war. Nothing was normal. They expected to be killed any minute. Anyway...' She took a deep breath. 'We were walking in the park. What with one thing and another I said I didn't want to see him again. I meant it at the time, and he knew I meant it.'

'Just like that? Didn't he try to change your mind?' Chris's sympathies were all piled up on his mother's side. He felt she was still letting the airman down too lightly even now.

'He did try, Chris. I'd run away from him, and...oh, it's a long story. He called back at the house, but I wouldn't budge. My mother tried to tell him I was pregnant and I stopped her. What a silly little thing I was.'

'No-' Chris said, but she interrupted him.

'I've always blamed myself for that,' she said. 'I'm sure he would have come back, and I would have told him...about you.

He was a decent man, Chris, don't you think anything else. He was sensitive...responsible. Everyone liked him. To let him go off like that...' She shook her head. 'The lives they led...they had to have something to believe in. They needed to be so focused on what they were doing. Any distraction, and...'

'What? What happened?'

'The next day he started training duties. That was the usual routine after finishing a tour. He took a plane up with a group of Australian pilots. It crashed.'

'And...' he said, bewildered. She had relayed it so simply, as if that brought the whole story to a close.'

'I know,' she said. 'I felt like that when it happened. There had to be more. But there wasn't. Suddenly it was ended. I never knew any more.'

'There must have been.'

'It was the war. I know I keep saying that, but people were being killed all the time. It was...nothing special.' She made a strange sound, half laugh, half sob. 'I didn't even hear about it for two weeks. There was a funeral of course, near to where he lived. His parents were dead, so the aunt had to organise it. She was in her fifties then. A nice woman. She got my address from somewhere and wrote to tell me about the funeral arrangements - we have no phones in those days - but there was some sort of mix-up with the post. I felt so bad about that. He went to his grave and I didn't even know.'

Chris looked at his mother, who was twisting her fingers together compulsively. His own preoccupations seemed quite small compared to the bleakness of her life in those days. To have been so close to someone and then...nothing. With his child inside her too. He had the impression she was re-living events now for the first time in two decades; events buried too deeply, not properly mourned. Despite the pain it was causing he couldn't hold back his own impulse to know more.

'Is this aunt still alive?' he asked.

'I don't know. If so she must be in her seventies. She wrote a second time telling me about the funeral, and I wrote back to thank her. I didn't see her again. I should have stayed in touch if only for your sake, but...it was difficult.'

He assumed this was a reference to Reg. There were questions about that too, but his mind was still harking back to the crash.

'The accident, Mum. Do you know what happened?'

She shook her head. 'I'm sorry. They didn't tell you much in those days, even if you were a close relative.'

'At least do you know if anyone survived?'

'Oh dear...' She was still twisting her hands. 'I'm not sure. It sounds so feeble, doesn't it? I think his aunt did say something about that in her letter. One of the Australians may have come through. Maybe not though - he was badly burnt.'

'Oh! Was...was my father burnt too?' He couldn't help visualising the last moments of the flight, the panic in the cockpit, and afterwards men crying out in pain. He felt the first stab of sympathy on his father's behalf.

Susan weighed her words carefully before replying. 'They were all horribly burnt. Unrecognisable, the aunt wrote. I've always remembered that word. But...' she said quickly, 'They said your father was killed outright in the crash. The Australian pilot too. They were...well, the burning happened after they were crushed against the instrument panel.' She turned her head away. 'I never wanted to think about that.'

'No.' Knowing what he did about wartime aircraft, Chris knew he could visualise the scene more graphically than his mother. He tried to wrench his mind away from a vision of the cockpit. 'You said it was a Lancaster?'

'I'm fairly sure about that,' she said. 'Though - you know me. I'm not very well up on planes.'

'Mum - do you know where it took off from - the flight that he died in?'

She thought. 'Bass...Bass something.'

'Bassingbourn?'

'I think so. That sounds right. Do you know it?'

'It's in Cambridgeshire. I've never been there.'

'I think that was it.'

'And do you know where the crash was?'

'I'm sorry.'

'Nothing at all?'

'No. I'm sure I never knew about that.'

He thought for a moment. 'Do you have any documents about the crash? Did you keep anything at the time?'

'I never had anything. Any papers would have been sent to his next of kin - that would be his aunt. I might be able to find her letters to me, but that's all.'

'I'd really like to see them.'

'I'll look. I'm sorry it's all so vague, Chris. At the time everything was horribly clear, and then...eventually you have to start a new life and put away the past. I know it sounds odd but that's what people do. They have to.' She stood up and took his hands in hers. 'You're not going to dig it all up again, are you? Best to let things lie.'

'I don't know,' Chris said, but he did know. Already ideas were forming about what to do next.

'It'd be so painful for your father - I mean, Reg.'

He turned on her. 'Would it? Don't you two ever talk about it?'

'Never,' she said, with an emphasis that was entirely uncharacteristic.

'And you, Mum - do you think about it sometimes?'

She looked away. 'It was all a long time ago.'

She took a tissue from the box on his table and blew into it with great determination, as if to say 'That's the end of that chapter'. Chris sat on the corner of the Liberator stand and gazed into the miniature cockpit. What had it been like in that cockpit in the seconds before they crashed? He longed to know more about it. He felt pretty sure that he'd want to probe into what had happened, if only he could find some sort of lead. He also felt - despite what she had said - that his mother would not really mind, at least not on her own account. She had suppressed the details for too long. Reg was another matter.

There were things he wanted to ask about Reg. (How easily his mind had transposed the old 'my father' to 'Reg', he thought.) At the same time he wasn't sure his mother could take another dose of emotion straight on top of the last hour. With another hint of the telepathy that sometimes surfaced between them Susan was thinking along the same lines, and offered to make a cup of tea.

'Another one?' he said. 'You've already made one this afternoon. I'll do it.'

'No - let me. Special occasion cup,' she said, almost jauntily, and went off downstairs. He guessed that she was keen to keep him and Reg apart for a little longer.

It was good to have a short break to think, but when she returned with the tea he plunged straight back in. 'Tell me about Reg - how you came to marry him.' He was wondering how much family history would have to be re-written in the light of these revelations.

'All right,' she said, cup in hand. 'Let's take things in order. First - you were born.' She smiled at him. 'And that was a very happy day, never mind all the complications.'

'Was it difficult?'

'You have no idea what it was like in those days to have a child...'

'Out of wedlock,' he said, parodying a scandalised tone.

'I'm afraid so. I'm sorry about that too.'

'I don't give a damn,' he said.

'Good.' She gave a rueful little smile. 'Things have changed, thank goodness. But actually, my parents were very good about it. I was so grateful to them. We went away to Northampton for several months, to your Aunt Doris. There was a low-key christening up there.'

'Oh yes - the names you chose for me. Christopher John?'

I liked 'Christopher'. As for John...' She sighed. 'Well, he *was* your father. His parents were dead, no brothers and sisters. I thought it was a way of...keeping a part of him, for you.' For me, Chris thought, or for you? She went on in a stronger tone of voice. 'When we did go back to Edmonton - with you in tow - it was a nine-day wonder in the neighbourhood, but they soon got used to the idea. It was-'

'It was the war,' said Chris, and they both laughed.

'Well it was. Not long after that I met Reg. His mother was a friend of my mother's - you know about that already. His first wife had died very young, leaving him with Alison as a baby.'

'Of course,' said Chris, suddenly struck by a new thought. Alison. She's not-'

'She's not your half-sister after all,' his mother interrupted. 'You have no blood-line in common. And yet you get on so well.'

'We do.'

'Anyway - there we were, Reg and I, both on our own with a young baby. In a similar position, in a way. All the same it was good of him to take me on, you know. People were very funny about unmarried mothers in the forties. He was good to me - and to you.'

'I suppose so.'

'Try to get on with him, Chris - especially now. Tell him things. He's more sensitive than you think. Please try.'

'I'll try for you, Mum.' He didn't need to tell her they'd never got on - could never get on. He knew why now.

They sat and talked for quite a while longer, trying to feel their way into the new landscape. Eventually Susan got to her feet.

'I'd better make some dinner,' she said. 'Heaven knows what. Cold meat and chips I suppose.'

'No pudding?'

'Pudding? What's that?' She breathed in deeply. 'What an afternoon. I've been dreading it for years.'

'Wasn't so bad.'

She came forward and kissed him. 'Nothing will change, you'll see. It's just a question of getting used to things. Reg has been telling Gary while we've been up here. I'll let Alison know all about it when she gets in.'

'There is one thing,' Chris said, as she turned to leave. 'Do you have a photograph of him?'

'Oh...I don't think so.' She looked flustered and he knew it wasn't the truth. His mother had always been hopeless at lying.

'Mum...?' He gave her a very direct stare.

'Well, I'll have a look,' she said. 'Maybe there's something.'

~ Four ~

16 September 1944

Gregson slept for six hours, waking more than once in that time to hear the imagined sound of the Lancaster's engines roaring in his ears. He rose feeling unrefreshed and went across to the mess for lunch. The end of the tour had left him feeling bemused. It was new and strange not to have a bombing run lined up for the immediate future; not to have the imminent prospect of dying. Already he could sense a disparity between himself and some of his colleagues. A pilot whom he knew slightly, and who was flying that night, sat at a nearby table with the absorbed, mechanical air that Gregson recognised from his own manner during the previous weeks.

After lunch he telephoned Sarah Frielen's guest house and, finding her out, left a message with reception, saying that he would call at seven that evening. Then he wrote a letter to the parents of Dave, his dead gunner, needing two trial versions before he had one he was willing to use. After that he sat on the bed with his back to the wall reading a novel, and waiting for the time to come round when he could call on Sarah. It was odd for him to have time on his hands; pilots had little space in their lives for anything but eating, sleeping and flying.

That evening, when he got to the guest house at seven, Sarah was in the small reception area waiting for him. She was talking to the landlady - a woman with a comfortable figure and a lot of make-up on her face - who looked up curiously as Gregson entered.

'You got my message, then?' Gregson said to the actress, shaking hands rather awkwardly.

'Joan here passed it on to me. I was glad you could come.'

'Of course I came.'

They stood for a second or two looking at each other. In a way he felt that he was seeing her for the first time; ten days ago she had been wearing stage make-up and playing the part of someone else. Even so he would have recognised the actress from the way she stood: confident, relaxed, staring openly at the airman and not fazed by his own patent embarrassment. She wore a pale cotton dress that was a lot nicer than the clothes most women could lay their hands on during war-time. Her dark hair fell onto its shoulders. He noticed now that the skin of her face was rough and pitted, as though she had once suffered from a mild attack of smallpox, yet if anything this enhanced her attraction. Her eyes were black; she could have passed for a gypsy. When she smiled, her features took on an expression that was almost wolfish.

It seemed natural for her to take the initiative. 'What did you think - about my idea of having a meal?'

'Yes...that's fine by me.'

'Do you know the Berndes Grill?'

'Well...actually, I don't each out much...usually.'

She laughed. 'That's because the country stuffs you airmen with all the finest food that's going. Come on - I'll introduce you to the place.'

'Right then.' He still hung back, feeling awkward about something else. 'As long as...well, as long as I pay the bill.' Already this was getting tricky. He did not know what class of restaurant she had in mind, and airmen were paid a pittance. She was ready for that too.

'But I invited you, John. Let's not stand on ceremony.' She took his arm lightly. 'Go Dutch?'

'OK.' He was relieved. 'Thank you.'

They walked into town. Sarah had a confident, almost prancing way of moving along, and Gregson was aware of several heads turning to look at them. They would be thought of as a couple, he realised: a tall airman in uniform and a dark-haired woman alongside him. The thought increased his sense of embarrassment, of being out of his depth. The whole experience - going out with a woman he didn't know - was outside his normal routines.

The restaurant was a small establishment just off the centre of Cambridge, of the kind he would not normally frequent. Some standard wartime notices decreed that patrons could not order more than one course, and that the cost of a meal should not exceed ten shillings. The place was half full; the customers looked more than usually well-heeled, and he saw only one other airman in uniform. Sarah was clearly known there and had reserved a table in the corner of the room. She ordered quickly, as though the food was of no importance, and he picked something at random from the menu.

When the waiter had left them Sarah gave Gregson a deliberate, appraising stare. 'Well now,' she said, 'What have we here?'

The pilot was entirely unaccustomed to such directness from a woman; unaccustomed, for that matter, to any woman's company but Susan's. 'So what *do* we have?' he said, gazing down uncertainly at the table cloth.

She sat back and ran her eyes very slowly over him again before replying. 'Well...a pilot, in uniform. A young man - perhaps twenty three, twenty four...'

'Twenty two,' he said.

'Tall, about six feet, dark, and - well, I have to say it - good to look at.'

'Stop...' he said, blushing furiously.

'Dark, curly hair, very thick. Sallow skin. Serious expression. And - I think - a sensitive individual, though it's hard to be sure on such a brief acquaintance.' He wriggled under her continued scrutiny. 'Very attractive hands, anyway, which is usually a good sign.'

'You must stop this,' he pleaded, 'Or I shall start on you.'

'Ah, but I already know what I'm like,' she said immediately.

He couldn't help being fascinated by her. 'And you think I don't?' he said.

'Maybe you haven't thought too much about yourself up to now,' she said slowly. 'Or not expressed what you think, anyway - even to yourself.'

He had the sense that she knew more about him than he knew himself. Perhaps it had to do with her looking like a gypsy. He half expected a pack of Tarot cards to come out of her handbag.

'Things haven't been easy,' she went on. 'You've had to struggle for what you want. You come from a working class family, I expect.'

'You know I do.' The pilot spoke very correctly, as far as grammar was concerned; his parents had been particular about that. Nevertheless something in the light, slightly nasal tone of voice signalled his origins.

'Tell me about your family.' She swayed back to make room as the waiter brought their food. Gregson looked at his plate without much enthusiasm.

'All right.' He welcomed the chance to divert her from direct scrutiny of his character. 'I was brought up in North London, near Finsbury Park. My father used to be a house painter. He died recently, after an illness. My mother's dead too.'

'Brothers and sisters?'

He shook his head. 'I'm very short of relatives. I have an aunt - my mother's sister. She lives quite near us.'

'And what about you?' she said, still in the role of inquisitor. 'Who are you? What do you like?'

Because they did not know each other, he found it easier than usual to be honest. 'I'm nobody special. Just another working class boy.'

'I doubt that. I want to know more. What drives you? What are you good at? Apart from flying a plane, that is.'

He shrugged. 'I was always good at maths in school. And making things...fixing machines, and so on. I badly wanted to be a pilot - otherwise I might have made a good flight engineer in the force. Like Freddy.'

'Freddy?'

'You know. Big moustache. We visited you together, in your dressing room.'

'Oh yes, Freddy...' She looked a little embarrassed at forgetting him. 'You meet a lot of people in my job. It was you I remembered.' The way she said this, giving her direct stare, made her suddenly seem more serious.

'I could still do the engineering side, at a pinch,' he went on quickly, dragging the conversation back to safe ground. 'It's something that comes naturally. I'm very careful about checking the plane before we do a trip. I think that's one of the reasons we've survived - so far.' From habit, he reached down to touch the wooden leg of the table. 'The mechanical stuff often comes in useful. There was a problem a couple of weeks ago, when I heard a blip in one of the aircraft's engines. I just knew there was something wrong. Refused to go up. They grounded me. Actually they locked me up at the base.'

'That seems a bit extreme.'

She had finished her meal, and he was showing little interest in his.

'I can understand their point of view, in a way. You get some chaps who'll do anything to avoid a dangerous flight. Invent some technical fault or other - go back to base. They call it "lack of moral fibre".'

She wasn't really interested. 'Not so bad as being a deserter,' she said lightly.

'Don't.' His expression had darkened alarmingly, as though she'd committed some dreadful social gaffe. 'Don't even think about that. Desertion is utter disgrace.'

'Sorry.'

'It's all right. We're a bit sensitive about that in the air-force. But the time I mentioned,' he went on, 'When they locked me up...I was exonerated. After a few hours someone came down to the guard room and said "You're in the clear. They've found a screw driver in the engine".'

'So there could have been an accident...if you hadn't spotted it.'

'It was possible.'

The waiter came back but she said she didn't want coffee. 'Maybe at my hotel.' She gave another of her piercing looks and leaned forward in her chair. 'I'm going to be very direct with *you* now,' she said.

He laughed openly at that. 'For a change,' he said.

'I'm sorry. Blame it on the war. There seems to be so little time.' She smiled, and again he noticed the wolfish expression. 'Do you have a girl friend, John?'

Gregson rocked back in the restaurant chair, as though his aircraft had been hit by flak. 'That *is* direct.'

'I told you.'

He wasn't sure how to go on, and she broke the silence. 'Will you tell me about her?'

No-go areas didn't seem to exist where Sarah was concerned. He found he could talk even about that. 'She's my age. Quite tall. Dark hair, like you. Slim. She lives with her parents and sister in a terraced house in North London - place called Edmonton. Even more of a dump than Finsbury Park. She works in a munitions factory locally'

'Hah!'

'No, that's not your cup of tea, I bet.'

'I didn't mean that. I meant you don't get much choice, as a single woman. You can get married, become a nurse, or help the war effort. That's why I became an actress.' She spread her hands disarmingly. 'Well...one of the reasons. So if you're in Finsbury Park,' she went on, 'And the lady's in Edmonton, how did you meet?'

'That aunt I mentioned - my mother's sister - she lives in Edmonton. We visited her one Sunday and went to morning service. She was there.'

Sarah seized on this. 'That's something else about you then. You're a church-goer.'

'I always have been,' said Gregson shyly. 'All my family. I was in the church choir before this business started. What about you and church?'

She simply stared, and they both laughed.

'Well on second thoughts, perhaps not,' Gregson said.

'What's her name?' Sarah said suddenly, very quietly.

For some reason this revelation seemed like a betrayal when the other details hadn't, but Gregson still said it.

'Susan.'

'And are you engaged or anything like that?'

Perhaps it was because the question was difficult to answer, but for the first time the pilot began to resent her intrusive style. He started to speak, stopped, and lowered his head.

Sarah reached forward and put the tips of her fingers on his hand. 'I am sorry, John,' she said, and seemed to mean it. 'Forget that I said that, please. I'm sorry to have intruded.'

'It's all right. Not really your fault.' He was still stumbling over words, yet more of them came out. 'It's just that things aren't straightforward,' he heard himself say. 'We've agreed to become engaged but not told anyone.'

'Oh...then I'm the first to know,' Sarah said brightly, changing the tone. 'I feel honoured.'

'So you should be.' He stood up, taking the initiative for once, and closing the subject at the same time. 'Let's get out of here. I think we've outlived our welcome with the management.'

Outside on the pavement she said 'Will you walk me back?'

'Of course.'

Above them the sky was heavily overcast. A good night for avoiding fighters, he thought. The streets were very dark, because of the blackout. They hardly saw a vehicle and there were few people about. As they walked Sarah slipped her hand over the pilot's arm. It was a casual enough gesture, but he was very conscious of the pressure of her fingers. He realised he was enjoying the experience, walking in the darkness with her beside him.

'What do you...?' she began.

But Gregson was determined to divert the conversation, to get himself out of the headlights. 'We've had far too much about me,' he said. 'You've told me almost nothing about yourself. Isn't it difficult, finding theatre work during the war?'

'Oh, no,' she said. 'Quite the reverse. This is the golden age of repertory, with so many London theatres closed down. It'll be more difficult finding work after the war - especially for a moderate actress like me.'

'I'm not having that...' He began to protest but she stopped him.

'I know my limits, John,' she said. 'That's one of my virtues. I'm confident on stage and quite nice to look at, but my acting doesn't have much depth.'

Normally shy about prying into the lives of others, he felt emboldened by her openness. 'And what about you and boy friends, Sarah?'

'I've had casual friendships with men,' she said immediately, her replies as direct as her questions, 'But nothing serious.' She stopped on the pavement and looked up at him. 'Until now, of course.'

Gregson blushed again. He'd enjoyed the evening - that was undeniable - but the thought of becoming involved with her hadn't entered his head. He had no idea how to take her comment. For that matter he'd no idea how to deal with her at all. It was as Freddy had warned: Sarah was outside his limited experience of women. The sense of strangeness wasn't only a matter of her background, though she clearly came from a well-heeled family, the sort he'd never known. It came from her head-on approach to life, her flouting of conventions. She left him floundering.

'You don't think I'm serious, do you?' she persisted.

'What about your leading man in the play?' he said lightly, trying to pretend she had not said it. 'He seemed the sort of bloke who'd be attractive to women.'

'Gary?' She looked up, amused. 'Oh, no. I'm not his sort of thing at all.'

'What do you mean?' Gregson was puzzled.

'You'd soon find out, John, if you worked in a repertory company. Most of the chaps are...well, not really chaps at all.'

He stared at her.

'I mean,' she went on, 'They prefer other men to girls.'

'But...how...?' He took time working it out, as she regarded him with raised eyebrows. 'But isn't that illegal?' he said at last.

She stopped again and leaned up to him. 'It is, but they still do it,' she whispered. 'Aren't the illegal things the most fun?'

When they reached the hotel she said 'Would you like to come up for that cup of coffee? I'm allowed to use the kitchen.'

'Don't the house rules forbid it?' Gregson had never been invited to a girl's hotel room but he knew airmen who had, and they usually fell foul of the landladies.

'You saw Joan - my landlady. She was an actress herself once. She's very liberal about visitors.'

There was no answer to that. Sarah led him up the dark stairway and opened the door of her room. She crossed to the window and arranged the blackout. When the light was switched on Gregson saw a typical guest house set-up, with a single bed, upright arm-chair, and wash basin. 'Cheerless' would have been too fulsome a description.

'Just a moment,' she said, moving quietly out of the room. The pilot thought she was fixing something to drink, but when she returned a couple of minutes later her hands were empty.

'I thought you were doing the coffee,' he said. For some reason Gregson's heart was hammering against his chest.

She took a step forward and pressed the full length of her body against his, looking up into his eyes. He felt her power invade him, as though she were a hypnotist.

'I don't want any coffee, John.'

She put her mouth up to his and immediately parted her lips and drew him into a deep, prolonged kiss. Standing there in the close confines of the room, holding her confident body in his arms, he was disconcerted but also felt a tremendous excitement. Freddy had been right: he was an innocent. But then no girl he'd known had behaved remotely like Sarah.

If her first approach had taken him by surprise, what she did next was a shock. Pressed against the outline of her figure he could feel his own body responding, and was embarrassed to know that she could feel it too. 'Oh!' she murmured, 'I ought to do something about this,' and before he could resist she was unbuttoning him and slipping a hand into the blue uniform trousers. The delicate machinations of her fingers brought a gasp from his throat. He made no effort to stop her - still less so when she took his hand, lifted the hem of her dress and placed his fingers between her thighs. To his astonishment he felt no clothing there, apart from the hard edge of a suspender; she was naked beneath the cotton dress. The tops of her thighs were slippery with moisture.

'It's all right,' she said a little breathlessly, as he hesitated. 'It just means I'm excited too. Sit down there, why don't you.'

She pushed gently with her free hand until he subsided into the upright armchair immediately behind them and, before he could stop her, moved quickly forward to sit astride him, modestly covered by the dress. The pilot gasped again but no force on earth could have persuaded him to deter her now, and he lifted his face as her parted lips moved to and fro a few inches from his.

For a few moments she arrested these movements, averting her face and gasping as though in pain; he became alarmed, in spite of his own swirling excitement.

'Are you all right?' he whispered.

Her eye-lids were fluttering madly, but she smiled down at him. 'I'm more than all right,' she said breathlessly. 'I just came.'

He stared at her, not wanting to betray his innocence; he'd not known that women could 'come'.

She settled herself more deeply on him, breathing heavily. 'And now you're going to come inside me.'

She began to move again and immediately it happened, and he lay back as the years of repression, ignorance and fear flooded out of him. He saw through his tears Sarah swaying above him - and for a moment saw too Susan's willing, confused face on another occasion. He stayed still for a long time with Sarah's lips against his neck, trying without success to think clearly.

Finally Sarah disentangled herself from him, straightened her dress and went downstairs to the kitchen. After a few minutes she returned with two cups of coffee. As she entered the room Gregson automatically stood up; the effect of years of conditioning.

She grinned. 'Now I feel like royalty.'

He grinned back, sheepishly. 'I'm just not used to being alone with a woman,' he said simply. 'Especially not in her bedroom.'

She gave him her stare. 'Maybe you could get used to it.'

They sat drinking the coffee, talking little, and then Gregson stood and said awkwardly, 'I suppose I'd better be going.'

'Please don't,' she said. 'You don't get away from me that easily, you know.'

He checked his watch. 'It's past midnight. The landlady...'

'I told you - it's not a problem.'

The pilot stood uncertainly by the door. He could actually see himself leaving - descending the stairs and walking away down the street - but his legs didn't move.

'Will it be a problem if you don't return to base tonight?' she asked.

'Well, no...it's not that.'

'Will you turn that light off for me, John?'

He plunged the room into darkness then heard her move across to pull the curtains apart. The window was wide open and moonlight poured into the room.

'I hate the stuffy rooms you get in the blackout,' she said.

He stayed there transfixed as she stood in the pale light, pulled her dress over her head and with typical, unselfconscious economy of movement removed her other clothes. He was struck by their quality, after Susan's makeshift garments. With that manoeuvre any resolutions he had about leaving were utterly confounded. She moved towards him and unravelled his necktie, unbuttoning the top of his shirt.

'Take off all these blue clothes,' she said, 'And come to bed with me.'

'You're going to be terribly disappointed, Sarah,' he said diffidently. 'I've no experience of this sort of thing...'

'I know,' she said. 'I'll show you. You're the only one I want to do it with.'

She was as good as her word, infinitely patient, showing him where to put his hands and how to move. During the night there could scarcely have been an inch of her that Gregson did not caress. There was a mole between her thin shoulder blades which attracted his lips again and again. He marvelled at his own stamina. Hearing her low moans of pleasure the pilot felt that he must at least be getting something right. And for him Sarah did things that he had never imagined in his wildest erotic dreams; she seemed to know all the things his body needed even before he knew them himself.

There was not much room in the narrow bed for two people to rest, and they spent little time sleeping. Once he did fall into a doze, dreamt deliriously, and woke to find her head under the sheet and her lips clasping him like velvet. They spoke seldom and did not need to speak, but once - in between bouts of lovemaking - she lay with her chin resting on his chest and talked with a seriousness quite unlike her usual, carefree manner. Afterwards he remembered these moments as having a dreamlike quality.

'I want to tell you something,' she said in a low voice. 'Will you listen to me, John. This is difficult for me. I know you're "almost engaged", but you're not engaged and you're not married and I think that entitles me to say this.'

'What? What is it?'

'I expect you think I'm like this with all the men I meet.'

'I don't...' Gregson's natural politeness conflicted with his sense of honesty. Her skills as a lover couldn't possibly have come from one or two casual encounters.

'I like being with men,' she went on, 'I'm not going to

pretend otherwise. And yes, I enjoy being in bed like this, as long as it's with someone I think is nice.'

Gregson lay there, slightly embarrassed, wondering what was coming. He was conscious only of confusion. For several years now he had felt, without reservation, that he belonged to Susan. Yet lying naked in this woman's arms he began to feel the pull of conflicting loyalties.

'That's what I've been like,' she said. 'I've had a good time, had some laughs, shed a few tears - not many. 'Until I met you.'

He tried to divert her by flippancy. 'Bowled over by the uniform,' he said lightly. 'Is that it?'

'You're not in uniform now, are you?' She giggled, and then became serious again. 'I've known men in uniform. What girl hasn't. No, John, it's about you, nothing to do with the uniform. And as I *have* had some experience of men you should concede that I probably know what I want - as far as any girl does.'

'We've only just met,' he couldn't help saying.

'Yes. I find it pretty hard to take in, believe me. I never went along with all that stuff about...you know...' She pinned him to the mattress with her intense stare. 'I'm a realist, if I'm anything. It seemed so far-fetched, falling for someone at first sight. And then it happens. I like you, John.'

He thought: she was proud of being direct, but now words were failing her. Could she mean 'love' when she said 'like'? Was that possible? They scarcely knew each other. How could she feel about him what he felt for Susan: that they were made for each other, that it was natural and right. He couldn't conceivably merit this passionate outburst.

'Don't say anything,' she said, putting a finger over his lips as he made to speak. 'Just hear me...if things don't work out for you...if you ever should need someone - for some reason, who knows - then come to me. I'll be here for you. Whenever it is. Don't forget what I've said. I mean it.'

'Thank you,' Gregson said, humbled by her intensity. 'I really appreciate that.' The formal response sounded absurd even to his ears. 'You realise I don't even know where you'll be? When does your play end?'

'Oh, this Saturday. Saturday's the last night of the run. Then it's all over.'

'And after that?'

'I'll go home. Stay with my parents - in the Lake District - until I can find more work. I'll give you the address.'

'Of course,' he said, aware that he wouldn't use it - and that she knew this.

When he finally left her it was six in the morning, and a grey light was invading the room. She rose with him and dressed quickly. They were both tired, almost exhausted, from passion. Everything seemed different in the dawn, as if someone had twisted a kaleidoscope. There was a heightened sense of things ending when they had just begun, and their moments together draining away. Gregson felt guilty and confused. He'd not even found time to tell her that he was moving on too, and quickly filled in the details of his training duties at Bassingbourn. He let slip that he was travelling in to London that day, and Sarah quickly divined that he was seeing Susan. She was in low spirits and her face looked ravaged. As they whispered goodbye she grasped his arm.

'John.' She seemed almost desperate. 'I know pilots usually take something with them on flights. Something for luck.'

He looked down at his feet. 'It's foolish, isn't it...'

'And I'm sure you have something of Susan's...of course you do.' She took some article from her pocket and hurried on, before he could interrupt. 'Look - I've got this blue garter. It's an actressy sort of thing, I know, but I wondered...from time to time, could you wear it? As an add-on? An extra slice of luck - that can't be bad.' She grinned in self-mockery but her eyes told him how much it meant. 'I'd like to think you might have it up there with you sometimes.'

He couldn't refuse. 'Of course, Sarah. Thank you. I won't ever forget tonight.'

She pressed her lips to his face as if her life depended upon it.

'I must leave,' he said, pulling free. Her door closed behind him and she heard his footsteps going away down the stairs.

~ Five ~

March 1964

Soon after his mother left Chris heard another tap on the door and Reg came into the bedroom. He stood just inside breathing quite heavily. It seemed an age before either of them spoke. Chris surveyed the stocky figure, the florid features with their crown of sandy hair, and thought: how could I have believed this man was my father?

'So.' Reg spoke at last. 'You know now.'

Chris nodded. 'Mum's told me everything.'

'I'm sorry.'

'It's nobody's fault,' Chris said. It didn't occur to him to wonder what, exactly, Reg was sorry about; least of all that he was sorry not to be the father of his 'son'.

'It's a shock for you, of course,' Reg said, 'But I hope it won't change anything between us.'

'No,' Chris mumbled. Change would have been welcome, he thought; a new start in an always-troubled relationship.

'I've always thought of you as my son.' Reg looked up at the Liberator model, and quickly away again. 'I'd still like to be...a sort of father, once things settle down.'

'We'll be OK.' Chris had his eyes firmly on the floor. He wished Reg would go away.

'I love your mother and I know you do too. I hope that's a bond between us.'

But Chris was out of civilised responses. He and his stepfather breathed different air.

'Well...' Still Reg lingered. 'If there's anything you need, whatever it is, I'd like to help.'

'Thank you.'

'Goodnight, Chris.' Reg came forward and put a hand on his stepson's shoulder. The unfamiliar gesture seemed forced and awkward. When Chris didn't react he turned and left the room, head down.

The interruption disturbed Chris's reflections about John Gregson, and he fell instead to wondering why Reg had married his mother. After all she'd been 'a fallen woman', while Reg was ever the guardian of public morality. During the sixties he'd never stopped jeering at society's marginals: beatniks, flower people, many other forms of (in his eyes) scarcely human life. Why had Reg departed from his own moral code to take on a disgraced single mother and - even less appealing - her child by another man? Chris knew one reason though it was not something he wanted to dwell on. With his room located next to theirs he sometimes heard echoes of their movements at night. He recoiled from the thought of Reg bashing away, red-faced, at his mother's slender body.

That was bad enough. But another question generated even more uncomfortable reflections: why did his mother marry Reg? He had often asked himself this without finding a sensible explanation. Knowing what he now knew the answer was surely very clear: his mother had married to give him, her son, a father and a decent chance in life. She had married in haste and repented at leisure. She surely wasn't, could not have been, 'in love' with Reg. She'd sacrificed herself for the son of her dead lover. Chris found himself centre-stage in a scene where he had previously been the innocent bystander.

He could not imagine how his mother must have felt over the past two decades, in a marriage to which she had been drawn by convenience rather than attraction. She and Reg were so different in every way. Reg had a jerky, bullish demeanour while Susan was light in her movements, like a dancer. Reg had strong opinions while Susan was diffident, rarely inflicting her views on others. Their interests were different too. Reg was preoccupied with politics and local affairs. His mother didn't really go in for hobbies or pastimes. She liked flowers, and 'going to the pictures', as she put it. She scarcely seemed to have noticed the explosion of television in people's homes, and preferred sitting in the local Curzon; Chris sometimes went with her because Reg never did.

'You're a long way away.'

Chris was so deep in thought that he'd not heard his mother come into the room. She was holding out an old photograph.

'Put it away afterwards,' she said, 'And please don't tell Reg I gave it to you.'

When she'd gone he looked at the snapshot with unexpected reluctance; an apprehension, almost fear. Not many people saw their father for the first time at the age of twenty-one. It was a black and white photo that showed his mother standing in a garden, hand in hand with an airman in uniform. She was smiling and seemed very happy. His father was laughing and had his head turned down towards the ground. He looked nice. I would say that, Chris thought, because he looks like me.

He gazed at the picture for a long time. He wanted more photos, dozens of them. The image on this one, yellowing scrap of paper was all he had to stand in for those crucial years: a woman shortly to conceive, an airman shortly to die.

He felt a pressing need to talk to someone not directly implicated in the chain of events. He phoned his girl-friend, Melanie, and spent ten minutes on the line. She was in the middle of some design work for her course but listened with sympathy; assured him she understood his wish to know more about the events of those days. He'd hoped Melanie might come round, but she had to finish off her assignment that evening.

Around eleven there was a tap on his door, and Alison stood outside.

'So,' she said, with a cheeky little smile. 'We're not brother and sister after all.'

It was a typical remark, from a girl with the knack of striking the right note in any situation. In she came, imposing her comfortable personality on the room. She had quite a plump figure for a girl of twenty-three, and it gave her a lot of trouble with mini-skirts. All the same boys liked her, and Chris could see why. Her face was round and very pale, with enormous green eyes which never seemed to blink. There was something unusual about her walk; she ambled along, scarcely lifting her feet from the ground.

Chris was always pleased to see her, never more so than now. 'What do you think about all this?' he said, more anxious than he had realised to hear her views.

'What a surprise!'

'You didn't know about it, then?'

'Oh no, Chris. No - of course not.' She seemed quite upset that he'd suggested it.

'Never suspected, just to yourself?'

She plumped herself down on the bed with a little smile on her lips. 'It doesn't take a genius to see that you and Dad are different. But then so are Dad and I, and I *am* his daughter.'

'Yes, and you're so much older than me. You really should have worked all this out.'

Alison giggled, and when that started it could be difficult to stop. 'I was all of two when we first met. I'm so precocious.'

They sat for a moment in silence. It was never a strain for him to do that with her. When she spoke again it was very quietly.

'You know, we're in the same sort of position, you and me,' she said. 'We each have a parent we're not related to. Does it matter, though?' I love Mum as much as any daughter could love her mother.'

'Yes, but...'

She gave Chris a look, knowing what was running through his mind. Alison was a funny mixture: a typical young woman of her time, which meant all the paraphernalia of the sixties, kicking over the traces, pop culture and the latest clothes; and a more mature, serene side, a much wiser head on her shoulders. 'Old before her time,' Susan had commented once.

'Dad's all right,' Alison said, with a look that almost implored Chris to believe her. 'Give him a chance. He's always been a bit nervous about you. I can see why now.'

'Do you ever think about your real mother?' Chris said, trying to change the subject.

'Sometimes. Not all that often. I've got photos, and Dad doesn't mind talking about her. Of course, I was only two when she died. And I had this ready-made replacement...'

'What about your mother's family?' Chris said. 'You're not really in touch with them, are you?'

'It's funny that, isn't it? I was taken to see them years ago, but I don't really know them. I don't seem to feel the need.

It's different from you though, because I know about them. There's never been a mystery.'

'I wish I could say the same,' Chris said. Thought I might try to find out more this Summer. Do a bit of research. What do you think? I don't want to upset anyone.'

'Yes, I think you should,' she said. The speed and certainty of judgement was typical of her. 'You need to know. And keep Dad on board as well as Mum. Don't make him feel out of it.' She stood and put a hand on his shoulder. 'And if you need a companion...I mean, if Melanie can't come, or something...I'd love to help.'

'Thank you.'

'Don't forget, then.'

They talked a bit more, and then she went off to her room, giving Chris a kiss on the top of his head before she left, as she always did. It had helped to talk to her. They would never agree about Reg, though.

Chris lay back on the bed and tried to make some sense of everything his mother had told him. The world looked a very different place already. He found it astonishing, knowing what he now knew, that he had never at any time entertained doubts about his origins. Reg - and for that matter, Gary - had always seemed like creatures from another country. But then it was easy to be wise after the event.

He began thinking of the task ahead, the business of discovering more about his father's life and death. It was going to take some time. The Summer was relatively free, apart from his work at the Hammer and Pincers - at least until the engineering course started in late September. He'd very little idea where to start researching for clues. It should help a bit if his father's aunt was still alive, and if he could locate her. Perhaps information could also be requested through the RAF. It might even lead him on to former friends and acquaintances of John Gregson, who could shed light on what had happened. Chris wanted to know where his father had crashed, and what had caused it. He wanted to know where he was buried. He wanted a better idea of what he had looked like. He longed to hear more about him as a person. There would be other matters too, but he couldn't be sure what until the hunt began.

There might also be things about his father that he didn't want to hear, but at that early stage he was scarcely aware of this as a consideration.

One thing he felt sure of: an interesting Summer lay ahead.

~ Six ~

17 September 1944

On leaving Sarah's guest house Gregson returned to the base, had a shave in his room, and went across to the mess to snatch some breakfast. He was in too much of an emotional turmoil to eat much, but he toyed with some toast, drank a lot of coffee, and pocketed a South African orange from a consignment that had just arrived for the flyers. He sat alone, glad that none of his friends chanced to pass by and join him. While he was there some of the crews returned from the previous evening's mission. They stumbled staring-eyed into the mess for their bacon and eggs, sitting in silent groups. He watched as though they were creatures from another world.

Back in his room, preparing to leave, he reflected that it was just as well Freddy had taken Bitsa for the night; the poor hound would have had a lonely time when its master stayed out all night.

Gregson got a lift into town and caught the first London-bound train, heading for Kings Cross. As usual there were too few carriages, and those few were packed with civilians - mostly women and children - and, amongst them, numerous airmen and soldiers. Gregson was lucky to get a seat in a corner, next to a woman with a baby on her knee and a small child sitting at her feet. The aisles were full of people standing crushed together. The luggage racks overflowed with the kitbags and pouches of serving men.

It was a warm day and the atmosphere in the carriage was stifling. Progress was painfully slow. At one point the train stopped for half an hour in a cutting. In Gregson's carriage the usual rumours circulated about possible reasons for the delay, and now these included the threat of the V1 flying bombs, the first of which had fallen on the capital a few weeks previously. Newspapers had been full of stories about the 'doodlebugs' as they had quickly become known. The pilot was only too well aware of them, since he had participated in several raids aimed at flying bomb factories in France. But despite all the speculation of his fellow passengers he was relieved that nothing could be heard to suggest V1 bombs passing overhead.

As the train carried him towards Susan he wished that it could have been on any day but this. He felt physically and mentally exhausted. He had slept poorly after the punishing last flight to Kiel, and scarcely slept at all in Sarah's bed the previous night. The prospect of seeing Susan so soon after stumbling from another woman's arms left him with a sense of impending disaster. Wartime liaisons were difficult enough at the best of times, as partners met and parted at infrequent intervals without the opportunity to settle into a steady pattern of behaviour. Both parties needed to be in good shape to make them work at all. Not that he had ever had any fundamental doubts. He had known that he wanted to marry Susan since the first moment of setting eyes on her, as she chattered in the aisle after evening service at Edmonton's parish church. Since then she had been the one constant in his turbulent existence. The sensation of her nylon stocking on the skin of his neck, on flight after flight over Germany, imparted stability and hope in equal parts.

Now, at the end of this tour, the reality of death had receded - for the time being, at least - and straight away he had made love with another woman. He was shocked at what he'd done yet in spite of himself he began, there in the crowded carriage, to imagine Sarah's skin against his and to hear her breath coming in short bursts against his ear. He could not relate what had happened the previous night to the one, brief experience with Susan in the Spring; their fumbling twenty minutes of passion had been more an act of commitment to each other than something to be enjoyed, as he now knew it could. Had he learnt something about himself last night? he wondered, though without illumination; something about the sort of man he was, and what he wanted from life?

He felt fingers tugging at his shoulder and opened his eyes. A figure was leaning over him, and it took a moment before he realised it was not Sarah.

'I thought you'd want to be woken,' she said. 'We've arrived. We're at Kings Cross.'

It was the woman with the baby and the small child. The carriage was rapidly emptying as its passengers spilled onto the platform.

'My goodness, son - you took some waking up,' she said.

He thanked the woman and helped to get her children off the train. 'You have a good long sleep when you get home,' she called after him in motherly fashion, as he trudged off trying to shake his head clear of fuddled thoughts.

At the station entrance the sandbags were back, piled high against the walls. After the clean countryside of Cambridgeshire the streets outside had an unkempt appearance, like the contents of a second-hand shop. Gregson plunged down some steps. Edmonton was not on the underground but he usually took a tube North as far as Manor House. The Kings Cross underground platform was littered with rubbish, and smelt of sweat and urine - further testament to the power of the doodlebugs, driving local residents back to nights spent underground. When the tube came, the short journey to Manor House was painfully slow; they twice stopped for long periods in the tunnel, leaving passengers to perspire in the heat.

At Manor House Gregson caught a bus, and sat at the front of the top deck as it ground through the familiar, drab suburbs towards Edmonton. The grey urban landscape stretched away in front of them unredeemed by any trace of greenery. There were few signs of recent bomb damage, though many of the buildings shattered in the early years of the war had not been restored. They passed the ground belonging to Tottenham Hotspur football club, where Gregson had spent many hours in his teens. He found it hard now to relate to his passionate support for Ted Ditchburn, Les Bennett, and the rest of that promising second division team. How important it had seemed then, and how trivial now. The ground still showed signs of damage from a blast sustained years before.

They passed the Angel at Edmonton, and Gregson alighted and walked through the terraced streets towards Susan's home. The rows of identical buildings of yellowing brick pressed upon him on either side. He felt more substantial than he did in the open countryside of Cambridgeshire, as though he dominated the narrow thoroughfares. There were few people about, although here and there a couple of women stood talking at their front gates, and looked up curiously as he passed; a pilot in uniform was always worthy of comment. With every step taking him towards Susan he felt more wretchedly unprepared for meeting her.

When she opened the door to him the doubts were confirmed. Something in his hangdog manner had immediately conveyed itself to her. Instead of her usual greeting, which always charmed him - one rapid step to swoop forward and kiss him - she turned half away with a muttered greeting.

'Oh, it's you.'

'Susan.'

He gazed at her, wanting to hear that everything was normal, but could feel the tension in the atmosphere. Unnerved, he took the South African orange from his pocket and pressed it into her hand, knowing as he did so that the action was ill-timed.

'Here. Put this away somewhere for yourself.'

She glared at it and turned away without comment.

It was common enough for wartime couples to get off on the wrong foot, especially after a long absence, but this was different. Susan was famously vivacious, and her rare bad humours generated a quick-fire anger which soon blew itself out. Today's mood was slow-burning and bitter. Her dark eyes were unfathomable and she barely lifted her gaze from the floor. Normally she almost danced her slim figure around the room; today she dragged about with sagging shoulders.

He followed her into the middle room of the house. Susan's sister seemed to be out, but her mother was at the sink in the kitchen. She looked up as he called a greeting but did not leave the scullery, and her response sounded less friendly than usual. What on earth was going on, he thought. Had he become a menacing presence overnight?; or was that notion simply a product of his own guilty imagination? It was almost as if the pair of them had received a telegram from Sarah, detailing the events of the previous night.

Susan went into the kitchen to make some tea, leaving him sitting alone in the tiny living room. Gregson had a working class background himself but these houses were a step down from the one he'd been raised in at Finsbury Park: three up, three down, poky, cramped rooms heated only by electric fires downstairs or - when it was available - coal piled up in the coalshed beyond the back door. The electrical wiring did not extend upstairs and the bedrooms were unheated, freezing in winter. There was an outside toilet and no running hot water, so that Susan bathed once a week in a metal tub in the kitchen, brought in from the garden. Gregson had always found it miraculous that her vivacious personality could spring from this unpromising setting, like a humming bird released from a covered cage.

She came back now with cups of tea. Her mother didn't join them and they sat almost in silence. Susan was wearing an ill-fitting dress which had clearly been put together at home from remnants of hoarded cloth. Again he could not help making a comparison with the elegant clothes worn by Sarah the previous evening.

'What's the matter with your hands?' he said. There was a bandage on one thumb and several fingers were puffy and discoloured around the nails.

'It's some sort of reaction against the chemicals,' she said. 'A few of the girls get that.'

He leant forward to take her hand in his, but she quickly removed it. 'But do you have to go on - with that infection?'

'They've taken me off the chemicals for a time. I'm an oiler and greaser instead.' There was a hint of her old irreverent spirit as she pronounced her title.

He looked up in surprise. 'What does that involve?'

'It means working nights, for a start,' she said. 'I go around the shop floor carrying a ladder and oil can, greasing the machines when the girls have their break.'

He tried to imagine her slight figure with a ladder. 'Isn't it heavy?'

'You get used to it. I'm not helpless.'

Nothing he said was right. 'You...you weren't working last night, surely?'

She nodded. 'Finished at six.'

He stared at her, taken aback. 'But you've not had any sleep then?'

'I got a few hours in. I look better than you.'

Perhaps it was simply lack of sleep, he thought - on both their parts - that was making their encounter today so hopelessly disjointed.

Susan's mother passed through the room from the kitchen, on her way upstairs. She threw a sour look at them but said nothing.

'Look - shall we go for a walk,' said Gregson, almost in desperation, feeling the claustrophobic atmosphere of the house pressing in on them. 'To the park, maybe?'

'All right.' She was up in a trice and walking to the door.

They went side by side through the back streets, but Susan did not take his arm. She wore her ill-fitting dark dress with a pair of flat shoes, and had her head bare. In the High Street the ruins of the bombed Alcazar cinema - which he and Susan had frequented early in their courtship - were just as he had last seen them. Edmonton was not a major target for German bombers, but the gas cylinders in Silver Street meant that the suburb got some attention.

'I tried to telephone last night,' Susan said suddenly. 'They said you weren't around.'

'What time was that?'

'Around ten. I thought you'd be in by then.'

'No. I was out.'

'At the pub?'

Susan wasn't a jealous woman, but he knew this to be dangerous ground. Yet, he found with surprise, he scarcely cared what came out. Part of him wanted everything in the open.

'No. I was eating out - unusually.'

'That is unusual,' she said. 'With Freddy?'

'No - with a friend. You don't know them.' The non-committal pronoun didn't reveal a female companion; it was a kind of lying, a new and uncomfortable experience in his life with Susan.

She left it at that and they turned through the park gates. Not many London locations could have had fewer points of interest than the suburb of Edmonton, but Pymmes Park at least provided a place of tranquillity for those who wanted it. The tree-lined paths were another reminder of early courting days. They turned down beside the pond, which was disfigured by a belt of scum on the surface of the water. A family of ducks went past, ducking and weaving.

'We need to talk, John,' Susan said, looking away from him across the water.

He glanced up uneasily. A heart-to-heart was the last thing he wanted. But there was no stopping her.

'I don't know if we're right for each other,' she said, still gazing into the lake. Her face was set in a way he had never seen before, so distant from her usual state of animation. 'I think we ought to reconsider the whole thing. Let it cool off for a while.'

Despite the ambivalence of his own feelings, he was staggered. 'What's brought this on?' he said, seizing her shoulders.

She shook herself free. 'We live in different worlds,' she cried. 'We can't possibly know each other properly, can we? You're likely to be killed most nights of the week...'

'Not any more.'

She ignored this. 'I can't even imagine what you go through. I know it's awful for you. But it's not easy here either. It's not exciting and glamorous. We're not in the spotlight like you. We just...go on. We get by. I know I look drab...'

'No, you look- '

'There's no chance to be anything else. We get by, if we're left alone. I don't need to be patronised. I don't need your oranges,' she cried out, absurdly.

'No...I'm sorry...' He could feel his eyes filling up.

Again he tried to hold her, but she tore away and half-ran from the lake and into the large open field where teenagers played football matches on Sundays. He trailed behind. This was the area where anti-aircraft guns had been situated throughout the war. There was much activity now around the edges of the field, with soldiers moving briskly about, some of them dragging one of the heavy guns towards a lorry parked in the street alongside. With part of his mind - the serviceman part - Gregson guessed this was a function of the national initiative to move guns to the coast, where they could be more effective against the new V1 missiles.

Apart from the soldiers, he and Susan were alone in the middle of the field. She had stopped running, and stood there looking slight and vulnerable. Gregson was at a loss as to how to approach her. Every move he'd made today had been misjudged or misinterpreted. There was something troubling her that he did not know about. Had she divined his own feelings of guilt with some species of female intuition? Or was it some other matter? Surely she had not found someone else too?

When he came near she seized him by the lapels, as if she were going to shake him. Now she did look into his eyes.

'Let's call it off, John,' she said. 'We spend so little time together. We can't lead a natural life like this, and I'm tired of it. I can get through all right if you leave me alone. You don't need me.'

He rocked back as though jolted by an electrical shock. For several moments he was unable to speak. There was no artfulness in Susan's character and he knew she meant what she said. He'd gone to Edmonton racked with self-doubt, but it was she who had spoken out. Now that she had put the thought into words he was overwhelmed by the idea of losing her. Seeing her there in the park, with spots of colour in her pale cheeks, he had never admired more her courage and unaffectedness, the sweetness of her nature.

'Don't,' he called. 'Don't say that.'

'I mean it. It's all wrong. It's the war, don't you see.'

The tree-tops round the edge of the park seemed to reel in the sky. Despairing, he seized her hand, and before he knew it the word was out.

'Sarah, please.'

There was a sick moment when the import of this sunk in for both of them. She turned back to him mutely, with a crushed expression. He made no attempt to dissemble or explain. None was necessary.

'Goodbye John.' She spoke in a voice heavy with resolution and regret. Her anger had evaporated. He felt the life he knew slipping away.

'Please, Susan. Hear me out. Now the words came. 'It was nothing. I met her once...'

'That's not it.' She didn't try to find out more about Sarah. 'It's about *us*, can't you see. I told you - we're not going to see each other any more. Please don't try to contact me. I won't do it.'

'I can't bear this,' he called out, as she turned away.

She stumbled on the rough turf, making for the park gates, and turned back for a moment. Tears were rolling down both sides of her face. 'Good luck.'

Gregson stood and watched as she ran across the playing field and disappeared from view behind a row of bushes. He could have gone after her, but felt he scarcely deserved another hearing. His opinion of himself was lower than any accusation she could bring.

He stayed for a long time in the middle of the park, head down, wretchedly unconscious of what was going on around him. When at last he did look up he noticed that soldiers around the AA guns were gazing at the sky. Then he heard it: a spluttering sound that might have come from a giant airborne motor cycle approaching from the direction of Angel Road. Gregson craned his neck upwards. An extraordinary sight met his gaze. Across the summer sky, with its puffy white clouds - at a height well below that of any normal aircraft - moved a large cylinder trailing a fiery tail. Despite his emotional turmoil he was intrigued to set eyes on one of the notorious new weapons. At once came the sound of the air raid hooter, in short, sharp blasts, warning of imminent danger. At the back of his mind the pilot was dimly aware that the spluttering sound had stopped. But he did not see the conflagration extinguished at the V1's tail; nor did he see the khaki-clad soldiers throw themselves to the ground on the far side of the playing field.

Before the deep roar blasted his ears Gregson was aware of a dazzling flash. He was never sure what happened next; whether he threw himself down or was knocked there by the force of the explosion. All he knew was that he was on the ground with his face in the grass. When he looked up the scene that met his eyes was one of unimagined devastation. A good seventy yards away, in a row of semi-detached houses bordering the park, he saw a building near him swell like a balloon before the glass shattered from all its windows. Some trees near the road were stripped of their leaves and stood with branches bare, as if in late autumn. A column of ash-laden smoke rose from the centre of the blast, behind the row of houses.

Gregson picked himself up. His hands were shaking and his legs bore his weight uneasily, but he seemed to be unhurt. Above the hooter an eerie wailing sound floated across the playing field from the direction of the shattered buildings. Realising that he was nearer than anyone else he ran towards them, clambering over the railings at the edge of the park. The road in front of the houses was littered with thousands of glass splinters. He stooped down to something in the gutter and recoiled, feeling his stomach churn. Forcing himself, he bent for a second look. It was a baby, horribly mutilated, but with its face almost intact. The infant could have been blasted through one of the first floor windows and disintegrated on hitting the ground. The thing - he couldn't think of it as human - was an obscene presence in this mundane stretch of suburban road. As Gregson stood undecided, a young woman burst shrieking from the house.

'Wait,' he called, stripping off his tunic. It seemed ridiculously important to him that the woman didn't see the child as he had first seen it. He bent to the gutter and wrapped the body so that the worst of the injuries were concealed by the blue tunic. The mother threw herself down, knees crunching the shards of glass, and cradled the parcel in her arms, weeping with abandon.

It was all too obvious that nothing more could be done for the baby and Gregson looked around, fearful of what else he might see through the choking dust. Soldiers had arrived on the scene, and some residents were emerging from the blasted houses. A woman came slowly out of a nearby doorway, dazed, carrying a young boy in her arms. She seemed unaware of the deep cuts on her own face, one of which had blinded her in one eye, and pushed the child towards Gregson.

'Help him.'

The boy was conscious but silent with shock. His left leg had been torn off below the knee and the stump was bleeding profusely. Gregson motioned her to sit on the kerbstone, where she held the boy on her lap. Here at least his first aid training could be put to some use. He removed his tie, fastened it above the boy's knee to form a tourniquet, and twisted to stop the bleeding. At this rate he would soon have no uniform left, the pilot thought grimly. White dust, drifting down all around them, settled on the wound. Gregson held the mother's arm as she murmured something over and over again. He stayed with the woman until auxiliary ambulance workers arrived to take care of her.

Helpers were everywhere now, and the injured were being assisted onto ambulances up and down the street. Auxiliary Fire Service workers were tackling a fierce blaze two houses away. Wardens, out with their whistles, had roped off the ends of the road, keeping a growing crowd of spectators at bay. Visibility had marginally improved as the dust began to settle, revealing more of the flotsam from the explosion. A child's toy boat lay on the pavement with its hull smashed.

'Are you all right?' asked an ATS woman, seeing Gregson with blood on his arms.

'I'm OK,' he said. 'Just trying to help.'

When he felt that no more could be done he moved away through the barriers. From the street corner he got a better view of the damaged area, and saw that the people he had attended to were the lucky ones on the periphery, those with a chance of survival. Further back several houses were in ruins, and their inhabitants would surely be dead.

Gregson turned and made his way very slowly along the road bordering the park. He looked a strange figure, in shirt sleeves, the remainder of his uniform discoloured with dust and the blood of victims. Passers by regarded him curiously, but he was oblivious to their stares. Images of the dead and wounded would not leave him. The cries of the dead baby's mother reverberated in his ears. He was a pilot: one of the men who dispensed carnage like this upon German civilians, and was revered by his own people for doing so. He had seen that veneration expressed here in Edmonton as he sauntered in uniform past the terraced houses; small boys looking up at their mothers, pointed to their shoulders, to the wings they dreamt of wearing themselves one day.

Like many pilots he'd not - until now - had direct experience of bombing at the receiving end. While British civilians took this punishment he was in the air over Germany, releasing tons of explosives on the enemy's cities. Of course he had seen the devastation in the East End of London: the skeletons of buildings, empty window frames, rubble and twisted metal, shop fronts boarded up and houses abandoned. But these scenes were sanitised for public viewing, their victims nicely bandaged in warm hospital beds, or safely in their graves. The newsreels and photographs did not show the British public - least of all their heroic airmen - a baby's body in the gutter.

Still preoccupied, he turned into the main road near the Angel, where it was almost possible to believe that nothing had happened. Vehicles laboured under the railway bridge on the North Circular Road, and several queues had formed outside shops which offered some foodstuff in short supply. Rabbit? Sugar? Dried egg powder? Today their wait was to be in vain. Shoppers scattered as the air raid hooter started up again, and Gregson followed a stream of people making for the public shelter, near to where the brook ran under the high road. His mood was such that he didn't care whether he lived or died, but he followed the flow into the shelter and sat in the near darkness. A large, middle-aged woman carrying some potatoes in a string bag plonked herself down with a thump beside him, wheezing from exertion.

In the gloom he recalled the image of Susan running from him in the park. She had been going away from the V1 blast when he last saw her; probably safe, but he needed to be sure. It was a practical matter of checking on her safety, no more than that. At his present low ebb he felt unworthy of her. He would not foist his attentions upon her again.

When the all-clear sounded he left the shelter and retraced his steps to where Susan lived. Her mother answered the door. She stared at his bedraggled figure on the doorstep, but her expression was set and unwelcoming.

'Are you hurt?'

'No, I'm all right, thank you. Is Susan here?'

Briefly he saw the face of Susan's sister peer out from the living room and then disappear again.

'She's here,' said the mother, 'But I doubt if she wants to see you.'

'Is she all right, though?'

'She's not hurt, if that's what you mean.'

'A bomb fell near her.'

'So I heard.'

'Can I see her?'

She glared at him. In the past he had managed a decent relationship with Susan's mother, and she had been pleased enough to have a pilot visiting the house; there was a certain status attached to these things. Now he saw the other side of her nature. For the first time he noticed the heavy lines of discontent around her mouth, which betrayed how difficult she could be in the wrong circumstances. The old saw crossed his mind about a girl always turning out like her mother; though against this, Susan had often deprecated her mother's shrewish character.

'You bloody fool,' the woman burst out at him now. 'Can't you see...'

'Mum.'

Susan's voice came from the staircase, and in seconds she was thrusting her mother aside.

'You promised,' she cried, clearly very angry.

'For God's sake be sensible, Susan.'

'Mother, will you please leave this to me.'

Something about this battle of wills puzzled the pilot but there was no chance for him to pursue it. The mother retreated, muttering to herself, and Susan was left facing him on the doorstep.

'So you're not hurt,' she said.

'I'm all right. What about you?'

'I'm fine. As you can see. I'm not going to ask you in.'

'I suppose not.'

Her eyes were raw but she looked utterly determined. Standing here on the doorstep he realised that she had driven Sarah clean out of his mind, but it was all too late. Their futures were cast apart.

'I'd like you to go now,' she said.

He thought of all sorts of things to say, but none of them were right. So much had happened in a short time.

'I'm sorry,' he said, turning away.

'I wish things had been different,' she said, closing the door.

He went away down the familiar street with his face like thunder.

~ Seven ~

17 September 1944

The mess party was in full swing when Gregson walked in some time after seven. Tables and chairs had been pushed back against the walls and a melee of airmen was gathered around the piano, singing songs ribald and sentimental. The pilot stopped for a moment to take in the scene. All the WAAF girls at the base - and a few others besides - were present, but as usual their numbers were dwarfed by the mass of men in uniform. Beer had already flowed freely and the din in the room was overwhelming. Gregson's new training assignment - his 'cushy number' - had already changed how he felt about these oh-so-familiar gatherings. In an odd way he was almost a stranger amongst the strained faces belting out the hackneyed words as though there were no tomorrow - which in some cases would be an accurate and tragic projection of their prospects. Not a big party animal at the best of times, Gregson usually sat on the fringes at these events, having a quiet drink and thinking about preparations for the next trip. But tonight he felt like drinking; drinking himself into oblivion.

'John. Over here.'

Freddy was at the back of the room holding a tankard aloft, foam on his moustache. Gregson pushed a way through and gripped his friend by the arm.

'You OK?' The engineer gave Gregson a searching look.

'Not really.'

'How did things go in London?'

Gregson shook his head. 'Don't ask.'

Freddy assumed his 'I told you so' expression but refrained from pressing the point. 'I've got Bitsa outside,' he said. 'Shall we give him a drink?'

'What a good idea.'

They went out through the back, where the black dog - half Labrador - was waiting patiently by the door. He bounded up as Gregson appeared and slobbered over the pilot's hand. Gregson felt quite emotional at the warmth of the dog's welcome; something to do with needing affection, he surmised. He put his beer glass on the ground and watched the dog mop up the best bitter from it.

'Thanks for taking him, Freddy.'

'I'll always do that, old man...well - not for quite a while, it seems.'

'No.' Gregson pursed his lips. 'He's going to be lonely up at Bassingbourn - when I'm away.'

'You'll soon sort something out. I shall miss him. More than I'll miss you, of course.' The engineer gave Gregson another quizzical look and plunged on with the question uppermost in his mind. 'You saw Sarah?'

Gregson nodded.

'And?'

'Bloody hell!' The pilot shook his head slowly from side to side. 'You wouldn't believe it if I told you. I don't believe it. Even so, I don't suppose I'll ever see her again. That play we saw - it's finishing. She's going back to the Lake District - Grasmere, where her parents live.' He drew a deep breath. 'As for today...well, I saw Susan. It's all over. She's given me the push.'

'No, no no,' Freddy protested. 'She doesn't mean that, you can bet your life. It's the war. You know what it's like.'

'That was her reason too. But she seemed to mean it all right. I'll keep writing to her, but I'm not hopeful. She looked bloody determined.' He turned away, back towards the party. 'Wait there, Bitsa. Come on, Freddy - help me to get drunk.'

'You? You're never drunk. You've got an iron head. Famous for it, old man.'

'That's why I need your help. I mean to get drunk tonight. I mean really drunk. I want to feel no pain.'

'In that case...' Freddy ushered him back into the building. 'You couldn't have come to a better man.'

For a while they joined the congregation of airmen around the piano and sang out the old, familiar tunes.

> Roll out the barrel
> Let's have a barrel of fun...

Gregson downed a pint, then another - and then another - but still found himself remarkably sober. He wanted to blot out everything: Sarah, Susan, his bomb aimer's torn features, that baby in the Edmonton gutter. For some reason the image that kept recurring was the supercilious face of Coltishall's station commander complaining about his damaged runway. Something about that incident struck at the whole conduct of the war in Britain; left Gregson feeling marginalised, as though the thirty flights over the continent had counted for nothing.

Now his navigator Albert was up on a chair in the middle of the scrimmage, calling for quiet.

'Attention please...shut up, you lot,' he shouted, as the singing subsided by stages. 'I have an announcement. It's my solemn duty to draw your attention to a major event. We have amongst us...'

Albert broke off as a surge amongst the crowd dislodged him from his perch into the arms of the nearest airmen, whence he was restored, upright, to the chair.

'We have amongst us...a pilot who has just completed thirty missions...thirty, no less...'

A ragged cheer broke out to the accompaniment of some

chords from the piano. Albert continued his attempt to out-shout the noise. '...saving his best landing till last, destroying a runway at Coltishall...(cheers)...ten yards of fencing...(cheers)...and several head of cattle...(laughter and more cheers). You all know him - our skipper, John Gregson.'

Amidst the din of cheering and applause Gregson found there were tears in his eyes. I'm becoming maudlin, he thought. He'd not realised that he was popular.

'To celebrate this achievement,' Albert continued, John has immediately abandoned his crew...' (cries of 'shame') '...preferring the company of *Australians*...' A full minute was needed before the storm of abuse died down and Albert could finish his speech. 'Notwithstanding such behaviour...his long-suffering crew want to mark the achievement by presenting their skipper with this tankard...' - he flourished something overhead - '...for the use of himself or his dog, whichever has the greater need.'

A pewter tankard was placed in Gregson's hand, and before he could resist he was hoisted onto the shoulders of Freddy and Chris and paraded round the mess to more singing.

We'll meet again, don't know where, don't know when But I know we'll meet again some sunny day...'

After that there were some blurred intervals in Gregson's memories of the evening. He knew he filled the tankard several times, and presumably emptied it too. He thought he remembered Freddy on his shoulders as they jousted with Albert and Chris, but could not be sure. His most lucid recollections were of much later in the evening when some of the throng had dispersed. He was sitting on a sofa with Freddy, both of them in a much quieter frame of mind. Gregson was cradling the pewter mug in his hands and feeling absurdly sentimental.

'Shouldn't you be taking it a bit easy,' said Freddy, as the pilot poured some more beer down his throat. 'After all, you'll be going up tomorrow.'

''S'all right. Not till the afternoon. Got all morning to recover.'

'Even so.'

'You don't look so sober yourself.' Gregson twisted round in his chair. 'Do you ever think, Freddy, about what happens after we release the bombs on these missions. I mean, what happens down below...in Germany, or France, or wherever...'

Freddy looked at him steadily. 'I try not to.'

'I saw something this afternoon - in Edmonton, where Susan lives. A V1 went over...dropped on some houses nearby. It was awful - complete carnage. I thought...that's what we do...'

'I know.'

The pilot looked up sharply. The response had come in a strange little falsetto voice. Then the engineer hiccuped, and giggled, and Gregson realised that he was drunk; very drunk. Freddy's ample figure was shaking like a mound of jelly on a plate. The man had a well-known ability to cover up incapacity - at least, up to a certain point. 'You'll see,' said Freddy, returning his voice to the lower registers and stabbing with a fore-finger. We'll be the villains, not the heroes.'

'What d'you mean?'

'Banger...Bonger...Bomber Harris.' Once drink did overwhelm Freddy's defences they crumbled very rapidly. 'They don't like him, do they?'

'Who doesn't?'

'Churchill...the War Cabinet...the Cheesey Stuff...you name it.'

'The what?'

'The Chiefs...of...Staff,' Freddy reiterated, slowly and very deliberately, with a distant look in his eyes. 'Hard one, that. They don't like him. Harris...villain-in-chief. All changing, John. Invasion force are the new heroes. We're the villains - you'll see. Dropping bombs on civilians. Villains. Whoosh! I'm glad...I'm glad...I'm glad it's all over.' Freddy made an enormous effort to finish this last sentence, and fell face forward onto the arm of the sofa.

'Looks like it's time for bed,' a voice said behind him.

Gregson looked round. 'Hello Pat, he said.

The newcomer was Patrick Stephens, a young pilot from Northern Ireland. He was a slim, rather slight man, with a pale face and shock of vivid red hair. As usual, he was smiling; Gregson had never seen the Irishman looking anything less than cheerful. In fact Stephens had done a lot to overcome his unreasonable prejudice against men with red hair. Gregson knew him as one of the best pilots on the base - though the Irishman also had a reputation for the occasional wild outburst which sometimes got him into trouble with the authorities.

'Pat - would you do me a favour? Do you think you could give me a hand getting this man to bed?' Gregson asked.

'I surely will.' Stephens slipped onto the sofa beside him. 'But give me a moment first, John, will you? It so happens that I wanted to ask you for a favour.'

'Of course.'

'You're starting instruction duties at Bassingbourn tomorrow, aren't you?'

'That's right.'

Stephens grinned at him. 'Me too. Got my orders two days ago.'

Gregson stared. 'Now that is good news. So you'll be there with me.' He was genuinely pleased. 'I feel better about going to Bassingbourn already.'

'Very decent of you to say so.' Stephens's smile broke over his face again, as natural and irresistible as the sun emerging from behind a cloud. 'I'm pleased to have a friend there, too.'

'You said I could do you a favour, Pat. What is it?'

'Ah, that's the thing. I believe you're flying tomorrow.'

Gregson pressed a hand to his forehead. 'Tomorrow afternoon, worse luck.'

'That's what I heard. I'm not due to start till next week. I wanted to ask - will you take me up with you?'

'Are you serious?'

The red-head smiled ruefully. 'It's ridiculous, isn't it? You'd think I'd be glad of some days off. But I've never flown at Bassingbourn. I want to check out the lie of the land there. More than that, I want to make some observations about the Lanc's performance. Something I've been meaning to do for months, but you know how it is. When you're flying the kite in action there's no time for anything else.'

'I do know.' Gregson considered the request. This was typical of Stephens, whose 'wild side' concealed a highly methodical approach: meticulous preparation, checking of detail. They had similar philosophies for being a pilot and it was one reason they had both survived. 'It'll depend upon how many they want me to take up, Pat - whether there's a space.'

'Yes, of course. There's usually some spare room on these training flights. But if not tomorrow, some other day?'

Freddy stirred in the armchair next to them and slipped half out of it, so that his knees were on the floor and his head on the cushions. He looked as if he was praying.

'Look at him.' Gregson gave the engineer an indulgent smile. 'All right, Pat, you madman. It's OK with me. You'll have to clear it with the Station Commander, mind you.'

'I know that.' Stephens clapped him on the shoulder. 'I know what a stickler you are.'

'I doubt they'll object to having another experienced pilot on board,' Gregson said.

'Not when you consider some of the extra passengers who get taken up.' Stephens had a knowing gleam in his eye. They were both aware of what went on. The previous week one of the pilots had taken his WAAF girl-friend for a spin. 'Now then - do you want to shift this drunken disgrace of an engineer?'

Gregson said goodbye to the rest of his crew. He and Stephens hauled Freddy to his feet and, each taking an arm over their shoulders, frog-walked him out of the mess. The engineer seemed to be in a state somewhere between sleep and unconsciousness.

'Not time to get up yet,' he mumbled, as the cool night air found its way into his lungs.

Gregson called out for Bitsa, who bounded alongside as they manoeuvred Freddy's stocky figure through the base towards his hut. The dog thought it was a great game to have Freddy dragged along in this way, and circled round the awkward trio, more than once coming close to tripping them up. Outside the hut they found a couple of Freddy's room-mates having a quiet smoke, and persuaded the men to take delivery of the body. They lowered the engineer to the ground, bade him goodnight, and made to go on their way - only for Gregson to be called back.

'He wants you again,' one of the room-mates said. 'Says he wants to kiss you.'

'Of course,' Gregson said. 'How could I have forgotten.'

He dropped to his knees beside the recumbent engineer, who was still muttering 'kiss Gregson' under his breath; but Bitsa got in first, bounding forward and generously licking Freddy's face from top to bottom.

'Thank you, old friend,' Freddy mumbled. 'Goodnight, sweet pilot.'

'That was someone else,' said Gregson. 'Don't you mind who you kiss?' He leaned forward to embrace his friend, and planted his lips on the luxuriant moustache. 'Now you look after yourself,' he said quietly. 'And don't drink so much. It's not good for you. I'll get back to see you just as soon as I can.'

~ Eight ~

March 1964

Chris had determined that his first step towards discovering more about the fatal aircraft accident should be to try and make contact with his father's aunt. His mother had failed to track down the aunt's two letters, despatched to her twenty years earlier, so he fell back on printed directories of names and addresses. He had to hope that the aunt had not died (always a possibility, given that she was probably around 70 years of age by now), and that she had not married and taken another name. Since Gregson was quite a common name he also prayed that she had remained in London - and better still, in Edmonton.

He went through the London telephone directory, isolated a dozen Gregsons living at addresses with N9 or N18 postcodes (the two covering the Edmonton area), and began phoning round. The third number he rang was answered by a woman whose voice, at least, seemed to fall in the right age range.

'I'm sorry to bother you,' he said. 'I'm trying to trace someone. I was wondering if you once had a relative called John Gregson. He was a pilot - killed in the war.'

Chris knew immediately from the silence at the other end that he had found her.

'I'm Marjorie Gregson,' the voice said eventually. 'John was my nephew.'

He had given some thought to ways of introducing himself on the telephone, but not hit on one to soften the shock: the shock that he existed at all. It didn't help that he knew very little about the person at the other end of the line.

'I was hoping I could come and see you,' he said, putting off the moment. 'I'm trying to find out more about him.'

'Well...that may be possible,' said the woman. 'Could you tell me who you are?'

There was nothing for it. 'I'm his son,' he said. It was the first time he'd ever said those words, and his voice sounded a little strange as he did so.

He heard her intake of breath at the other end. 'I don't understand,' she said faintly.

'I'm sorry. I couldn't think of a good way of doing this. My mother told me about you. Susan. Susan Dilly.'

'Susan...'

'Do you remember her?'

'Oh yes, I remember her very well.'

'When my father died, she was pregnant...with me.'

'Goodness...' There was another, longish silence, which he didn't interrupt. He knew from recent experience what it was like absorbing information of this sort. When the woman spoke again her voice was different. 'What is your name?'

'I'm Christopher. Chris.'

'Well, Chris, I'd like to ask you to come and have tea with me.'

He took the bus down to Edmonton the following day. Going there was a journey of discovery in itself. Though the suburb was close to his own he knew nobody there and had had no reason to visit before. On a few occasions he'd been driven through it via the North Circular Road, but the associations were all disagreeable ones: choked jams of heavy traffic, close-packed terraced houses, and - all along Silver Street - the bleak marks of heavy and light industry upon the landscape. He could think of no reason why anyone would want to visit the place for itself.

It was therefore a pleasant surprise to find that Lower Edmonton had a different atmosphere from the area which harboured the main traffic routes. He had left himself plenty of time, and got off the bus at the Cambridge Road to walk down Church Street. The houses were quite varied architecturally, and the street gave almost a rural impression in places. At one point an old, stone cattle trough betrayed its rustic heritage. Half way down he came across All Saints Church, set back from the road in pleasant grounds. Here, he knew, was where his mother and father had first met. He walked through the green approaches and pushed open the main door into the church. It was still and silent, apart from the sound of hinges squeaking on the door. In the half-darkness the ranks of wooden pews stretched away towards the pulpit and altar. The scene would not have changed greatly in the past twenty years. Chris tried to imagine his mother and father in the aisle after a service, being introduced by the aunt and exchanging their first words together. Had that moment not occurred he wouldn't have been standing here now looking on.

Marjorie Gregson lived in one of the cottages at the foot of Church Street, separated from the main road by a compact front garden. The cottage next door had a blue plaque on the front wall announcing that Charles Lamb had once lived there. Chris could almost imagine the buildings over a century earlier, when Edmonton was surrounded by fields. He knocked at the aunt's front door. When she opened it he proffered the small bunch of flowers he'd brought, and she gripped his arm.

'My boy, you can't imagine what a shock it is to see your father reappear like this. You're so much like him, you know.'

He liked the woman immediately. Her features were weather-beaten, full of bumps and dimples and hanging folds of skin, but they radiated sympathy and humanity. She was slight, distinctly tottery on her pins, and - he guessed - not in the best of health.

They went into the living room, where she had laid out the tea things and some plates with cakes and biscuits. Everything was small, designed for one person. The milk jug contained just enough milk for two cups, then needed re-filling. She fussed about pouring tea and offering him food.

'How is your mother?' she asked.

He explained about Reg and his brother and sister.

'I'm glad she settled down. I liked her so much. Please give her my regards. I introduced them you know.'

'Mum told me. I've just had a look at the church on the way down.'

'They were both church-goers. People often were then. I think they felt they might die any minute. I don't suppose you...?'

'I'm afraid not.'

She grinned. 'No. I'm afraid I've let it go, too. One can be too serious. Your father was very serious, you know. He was brought up quite strictly. Church-goer, well turned out, always very responsible in his attitude. From what I saw, I'd say the RAF mellowed him quite a bit. I think perhaps he needed that. I even heard him swear once, after he joined the air force. Quite a shock. Now we can hear the f-word on television.'

'Yes,' Chris said. She seemed more liberated than anyone else he knew of her age.

'All those young men, from all sorts of families,' she went on, changing tack slightly. 'And the WAAF girls everywhere. They were quite free-and-easy, you know.' She stopped and touched Chris's arm. 'I'm sorry, Chris, I don't want to muddy his image for you.'

'No, it's all right,' he said. Her reference to wayward WAAFs made him think of the woman his mother had mentioned - the one his father had had an affair with. He'd almost got used to the idea now. 'I need to know about the real person,' he went on. 'I want to know it all. The good and the bad.'

She smiled, more to herself than at him. 'Oh, you won't find much bad. He was a very nice boy.' She was lost in thought for a moment, and her face darkened. 'Your poor mother,' she said. 'There was that awful mix-up about the funeral.'

'Yes. She felt very bad about it.'

'And with you inside her. It must all seem terribly inadequate to you now, Chris, but communications were so poor in those days. None of us had telephones. And of course, I didn't know you existed.'

'You were at the funeral?' he asked diffidently.

'I was one of the few who were. Your father suffered from an awful shortage of relatives. Mother and father both dead - no brothers or sisters. Some neighbours came. Most of his friends were in the services and it was hard for them to get away. The invasion force was off in Europe, of course. The RAF sent John's commanding officer. And there was a friend from his squadron who looked awfully upset. A man with one of those big Jimmy Edwards moustaches they used to wear.'

'I want to find out more about all that,' he said.

He had spoken with some passion and she glanced quickly across at him. 'Are you going to look into it?'

He nodded. 'I'm going to try.'

'Yes, I can understand you would want to do that. If you find out anything, Chris, I'd very much like to hear it myself. They told you so little during the war.' She heaved herself with some difficulty out of the arm-chair and went across to the window. 'Now I've put aside some things for you. Here are some photographs I had.'

She handed over at least a dozen snaps. Chris felt that Ali Baba himself had never set eyes on such a treasure trove. He leafed through them quickly: several rather staged pictures of John Gregson as a boy with his parents, two more with his mother, and some of him in uniform with other airmen. One large picture had his whole squadron arrayed under the wings of a Lancaster.

He'd have liked to pore over them for hours; but he gulped and handed them back.

'No - they're for you, Chris.'

'But they're yours.'

'They're yours now. Take them. I don't need pictures. I can remember John as if it were yesterday.' She reached into a cardboard box and pulled something else out. 'When an airman was killed,' she went on, 'They would send his personal effects on to the next of kin. I was his next of kin at that time. At least we all thought I was. None of us knew about you. It was very sad, having those things delivered at my door. There wasn't much, but...this was a bit of a surprise.'

She handed him a pewter tankard, yellowed with twenty years of non-use; on its side, an inscription: 'To John Gregson from his long-suffering crew, 16 September, 1944'.

'That date is just two days before he died,' she said quietly.

They were both silent for a moment there in her living room, with the Church Street traffic moving past her window. Chris saw two red Minis go by in succession.

'I hope you're going to take that away too,' his father's aunt said with a smile. 'I don't down that many pints these days. Now there's one other thing I thought you might like to keep. These were sent on to me a bit later.' She rummaged again and brought out two hard-bound volumes, astonishingly battered, looking like school exercise books - except for their covers, on which were printed 'Royal Air Force pilot's flying log book', with his father's name written in underneath.

'Oh thank you,' he said, like a child that had been given its most cherished Christmas present.

'You take those with you when you go,' she said, gathering up crockery. 'I'm going to clear away these things.'

Once again he appreciated her tact and understanding. She'd known he would want to take his first plunge into the log books without an onlooker. So it was there in her living room that he first saw his father's hand-writing: row upon row of entries detailing individual flights he had made from 1939 until the end of his career. Most were straightforward records containing bare details, but every so often the 'remarks' column recorded a description of some aerial encounter or unusual incident. Chris turned over the pages, which his father must have spent hours handling. They all had the immediacy of record.

He couldn't resist turning to the last entry, half way through the second book. Against the neat details in his father's handwriting - made in blue ink (no biros then) - was the shocking note in red by another hand: 'Crashed and fatally injured'. Below that an official stamp recorded dispassionately 'Killed on active service'.

The last entry in John Gregson's handwriting - in all probability, the last words his father ever wrote - stood out from the page: Date, September 18; Aircraft, Lancaster; Pilot, self; 2nd pilot, pupil or passenger, F/L Turner and crew; Duty, local flying. Chris stared at them. The bare record seemed unworthy of a man's life - several men's lives - and he felt once again the urgent need to discover more about what had happened. Here at least was a start: Flight Lieutenant Turner and crew; these had been his last companions.

Marjorie Gregson came back into the room. 'Have you seen your father's grave?' she said, without preamble.

'I don't even know where it is.'

'Would you like to go?' She sprang her surprises in such a gentle, appealing way.

'Do you mean today?'

'It's just down the road. We can take the bus.'

Again he was surprised by the spontaneity of her decision to visit the grave, something that would have been uncharacteristic in other people he knew of her age. Down Church Road the two of them went, to the bus stop. She tottered on those dubious legs of hers, but made remarkably good progress as he adjusted his pace to hers. The cemetery adjoined the Cambridge Road itself. Once there she led him straight to his father's grave - one of a small group belonging to airmen killed during the second world war - then, as she had after handing him the log books in her living room, wandered away a short distance to leave Chris on his own for a moment.

A simple headstone said 'John Gregson 1924-1945, rest in peace'. Other headstones stood in rows all around, like soldiers advancing in battle. The surrounding lawns were so brightly green that they might have been artificially touched up by artists. He stood there, almost to attention himself. The quietness was broken only by bird-song and the distant sound of traffic. The place was nearly deserted, except for a woman who knelt to lay a bunch of roses across the grave of a loved one nearby; and an old man in a raincoat who was slowly dragging himself along the path.

Chris had lived most of his twenty-one years unaware of John Gregson's tragedy. The influence exerted upon his life, such as it was, had been without his knowledge. When his mother at last revealed the unlooked-for news, there had been few signs that John Gregson had actually existed. One photograph, retrieved from a drawer where it had been concealed for 20 years. But there was no gainsaying the stone, with its simple message designating the remains which had once lain beneath; and still lay there, in their most basic, vestigial form. Here had once been his own flesh and blood. Even so the tears which now rolled from his eyes and down his face took Chris by surprise. He thought: I'm beginning to feel something for this man, whom I know nothing about. Or were these mere crocodile tears, an apology for mourning, two decades too late.

'It's not much,' said his aunt behind him, indicating the gravestone. 'It was the War Graves Commission style in those days - very simple. To tell you the truth, I couldn't have afforded anything more.'

He discreetly wiped away the traces of a tear before turning to her. 'It's a lovely stone.'

'I always come on his birthday, and put some flowers down.'

When they left the cemetery she suggested that she went home alone, but he insisted on accompanying her back to the cottage gate.

'May I come and see you again?' he said, out on the pavement.

'I'd like that,' she said in her measured way. 'I said your father suffered from a shortage of relatives, Chris. I have the same problem. It's been an extraordinary couple of days. All my family dead, and you parachute down out of the blue. I'm so glad.'

~ Nine ~

March 1964

It didn't take Chris long to discover that tracking down Marjorie Gregson was the easy part of his enquiries. All the log book had told him was the date of the crash and the name of the trainee Australian pilot; plus confirmation of the notion, only half-remembered by his mother, that the last, fateful flight had taken off from the airfield at Bassingbourn. The next steps were much less straightforward. He soon realised that his knowledge of second world war aircraft, picked up from modelling them over the years, was barely of any use at all. More to the point, he knew little about the way the RAF was structured, and even less about the labyrinthine ways of its bureaucracy, a feature that he soon saw was to be crucial. And on top of those layers of ignorance (which were daunting enough), he'd never in his life done any research of the sort he was now contemplating.

Given all these handicaps he was not really surprised when early investigations turned out badly. He spent some time trying to telephone Bassingbourn airfield, but found that getting information out of them was like extracting blood from a stone. All he could gather was that the base was now occupied by something called 231 Occupational Conversion Unit, which was mostly concerned with training air crews from other countries; these included (he noted this with a pang) the Australian Air Force, and it was a sign of changed times that the exercises had even involved pilots from the Luftwaffe. Months later he was to feel he'd been rather slow in realising that casual enquiries about operational air bases were not encouraged, to put it mildly.

Next he thought of searching local papers around the period that his father was killed. The reference to 'local flying' in the last log book entry suggested that the Lancaster had crashed not too far from Bassingbourn itself. He rang Bedfordshire Public Libraries and established that the paper covering the area in the 1940s was the *Biggleswade chronicle*, a complete run of which was available on microfilm at Bedford central library. One morning Chris took the train to Bedford from St Pancras station, and spent several hours crouched over an antiquated machine scanning issues for Autumn 1944. The procedure was uncomfortable (a friend had once described microfilm as 'the unpublishable in form of the unreadable') and dispiriting. The columns of the newspaper were close printed and, for that matter, dreadfully dull. After several hours of searching he concluded that there *was* no reference to the crash in the *Biggleswade chronicle's* pages; or if there was he'd missed it, and had no intention of going back to look again.

All the same the visit wasn't a complete dead waste of time. He got talking to a helpful girl on the counter and she went off to ask a Mr Brown, the Reference Librarian, who, she said 'knew a lot' about such things. Mr Brown, a little man who blinked persistently, reminded him of a mole making a rare excursion into the light, but he knew his stuff. He told Chris that news reports of RAF accidents were usually censored during the war, which was probably why nothing had turned up in the *Chronicle*. He advised that there was an RAF address which dealt with enquiries of this kind, and wrote down the details.

Next day Chris telephoned the RAF Personnel Management Agency in Gloucester and explained what he was looking for. A helpful bloke on the other end of the line said that provided Chris was a next-of-kin they could for a fee of £7 do a 'service record search', which would consist of personal details plus a list of squadrons served. It was not what he wanted but again there was a clue to the next step. Apparently details of accidents involving RAF aircraft could often be obtained from records held by the RAF Museum at Grahame Park, Hendon.

He phoned the museum straight away and was put through to someone in the research department. Once again the contact was more than helpful - a recurring feature, it seemed, of the people who looked into matters involving wartime aircraft. The man confirmed that accident searches were quite often done at Grahame Park, usually through an independent researcher who knew the ropes. Chris told him the little he knew about his father's accident and the man gave details of two people he thought might be suitable. Without even putting the receiver down Chris rang the number for a Christian

Smythe. Smythe himself answered the call. After a few minutes he had agreed to take the job on for a fee which seemed to Chris eminently reasonable. He sounded knowledgeable and enthusiastic - almost, it seemed, as though he could hardly wait to get started. Chris was beginning to realise that, even as late as the 1960s, wartime flying supported a small industry peopled by men who didn't really want to do anything else.

Smythe estimated that the work would take about three weeks, and during that time Chris could do nothing but wait. The time passed more slowly than any he could remember. To take his mind off things Chris busied himself with extra shifts at the Hammer and Pincers and preparing for his driving test. Every day at home he was first to the door mat to check the incoming post. After three weeks, on cue, an envelope arrived with a postmark from Cambridge, Smythe's home town. Chris took the letter up to his room and ripped it open.

At first the contents seemed disappointingly sparse. The envelope contained a bill for Smythe's services and a page of details. Some of these Chris already knew from the log book - for instance, that his father had a total flying time of over 2,500 hours. The notes also confirmed that John Gregson's last flight took off from Bassingbourn airfield, where he was on detachment from the base at Mepal for 'flying instruction duties'.

Then came the new information. First was a reported statement that the cause of the crash was not known for certain. The probable reason was given as engine failure compounded by what they referred to - Chris was mortified to see - as 'pilot error'. The training flight had been scheduled to explore 'flying on three engines', and the aircraft was said to be flying too low for the manoeuvre. The words 'pilot error', heavy with blame, glared out from the page. Chris immediately found himself searching for theories to contradict them; this was the RAF protecting itself, and there would be a built-in tendency to blame the pilot rather than the organisation; and as the report had observed, his father had 2,500 hours of solo flying at the time of his death, hardly the record of a man to take unnecessary risks. Arguments of this kind went round and round in Chris's head. He suddenly realised how strongly he was taking Gregson's side, rather than - as at first - blaming the pilot for what had happened to his mother.

Chris was starting to regret the commission to Christian Smythe when his eyes fell on the last paragraph of the statement. There on the paper were the simple words: 'Crash location: Potton Wood, Cockayne Hatley, grid reference TL255499'. An additional note described the crash site as being seven miles South East from Bassingbourn airport.

At last, something concrete to go on. He hauled the family road atlas from its berth in the book-case. Cockayne Hatley was right out in the sticks, just inside the boundary of Bedfordshire. The nearest place of any size was a town called Sandy, three miles to the West, with Bedford a few miles further on from that. The only wood near Cockayne Hatley - which he assumed must be Potton Wood - looked as if it was less than a mile across. On the map it constituted a green splodge smaller than a thumb print. It was here that his father had died.

~ Ten ~

April 1964

Chris needed all his willpower not to visit Potton Wood straight away to look at the site of his father's accident. Common sense prevailed, but only just. The map showed the wood to be fairly remote from urban centres, and he imagined that getting there from the nearest train station - Bedford - could be difficult. He decided to wait a week until he'd taken possession of his car, and also to find a day when his girl-friend Melanie was free to accompany him.

They set off on a mid-April morning that was misty and none too warm. It was the car's maiden voyage with her new owner, if not exactly in her lifetime (for she had 96,000 miles on the clock). Chris was keen to see how the old war-horse would respond to a longish journey. Everything seemed in working order apart from the right-hand indicator, which needed a good thump on the interior side-panelling before it would emerge from its recess. He'd christened the vehicle 'Clara'.

Melanie gave the car a critical glance when Chris picked her up from home. 'Don't know about this,' she said. 'I only travel in the latest models.'

'Look, this car has character,' he told her. 'And don't forget - if it weren't for Clara we wouldn't be going to Potton Wood at all. It was only because I needed my birth certificate for the driving licence. That's what started all this off.'

'And it would be tragic not to see Potton Wood,' Melanie said with a giggle. 'Who knows what delights are in store for us.'

If Clara was not one of the latest models, Melanie certainly was. Chris never tired of watching her move about, as now, for instance, settling herself into the ancient upholstery of Clara's passenger seat. She was nearly six feet in height, much of that taken up by her extraordinary, elongated legs, and dressed with the style that was to be expected of a girl on a design course. Her expression combined sophistication with (Chris had to admit) a barely disguised streak of carnality.

Since they'd met, a year earlier, Chris had been with her whenever he could manage it; or to be more precise, whenever *she* could, for the design course took up a lot of her time. They went to pubs and cinemas and (whenever Melanie's parents were out) to bed, which she described as 'her natural habitat'. She was the cultured one, dragging him off to concerts and exhibitions that would never normally have been considered. He felt she was good for him in that way. When he thought about it Chris supposed he was a little in awe of her. He couldn't quite believe his luck, attracting a girl with her attributes. The question he sometimes asked himself (without finding any real response) was what was it about *him* that appealed to her? He hoped it was something that would lead in due course to a more settled relationship.

It took about an hour and a half to get to Royston. Melanie wanted to stop there for a cup of coffee, but Chris was impatient to push on. Cockayne Hatley and Potton Wood had been haunting his imagination ever since they appeared on the researcher's report, and he could hardly wait to discover the reality behind the place-names. After Royston they entered a network of minor roads and at length, near a village called Wrestlingworth, saw the first signpost to Cockayne Hatley.

They were out in open country now, driving through stretches of cultivated ground. The landscape was essentially flat, but rose very gently before them. The villages in the area were sparse affairs. When Cockayne Hatley at last came into view, Chris wasn't at all sure the belt of houses straggling down the slope ahead would warrant a place name of their own. Only the spire of the church, visible at one end of the village, gave the place some significance. He drove Clara up to the church grounds, stopped the engine, and got out. The wind tugged at the collar of his jacket. It was quiet and there was absolutely no-one about. He looked around. This was the place, he thought, with suppressed excitement.

The mood evidently wasn't shared by his companion. 'Is it parky enough for you?' said Melanie, who had emerged on the passenger side of Clara and was hugging herself against the strong breeze.

Chris scarcely heard her. He stood gazing at a scene which, in all probability, was the last his father had ever seen. From the church, the land sloped away towards the dark stretch of trees (surely Potton Wood) a couple of hundred yards distant. This was farming country, and most of the ground was cultivated. Away on the horizon the shape of a tractor was just about discernible. Beyond Cockayne Hatley a few additional houses were dotted around the countryside and, near the wood itself, a farmhouse and a large water tower. That was all. The sound of the wind sweeping across open land increased the sense of isolation. In the distance someone was banging away with a hammer, and the noise carried unabated across the flat landscape. It was a lonely, almost a desolate scene.

They walked round the side of the church past a frieze of trees. At the rear of the building a scattering of grave-stones showed how few people had lived and died at Cockayne Hatley over the years.

'Not sure about the building as a whole,' Melanie said, 'But I'd guess the tower was fourteenth century, wouldn't you?' Chris made no response. She knew his ignorance of architecture; that he wouldn't have a clue about dates.

They tried the church door, but found it locked.

'What now?' she said, stamping her feet on the gravel path.

He heard a car door slamming. A short way down the approach road was an official-looking building with a parked car outside and a man bending over the boot. Chris hurried towards him, and the bloke looked up at the sound of footsteps.

'Excuse me,' Chris said, 'But do you know if there's a key to the church anywhere.'

'You'll find one in the office there,' the man said. 'Go through that door.'

Melanie trudged up behind him and they entered the building, which turned out to be the office for the whole estate. They were greeted by an agreeable-looking woman in her early forties, who handed over the church key when Chris made his enquiry.

'Just casual visitors?' she asked. 'Sorry to pry, but we don't get too many tourists out here.'

Chris hesitated. 'Not exactly. My father was killed in Potton Wood towards the end of the war. I've only just found out where it happened, and we came up to see what the place was like.'

The woman gave him a hard look. 'Again, please forgive me for asking, but was it about the plane crash?'

'That's right,' he said. 'My father was the pilot. Do you know about it?'

'Everyone up here knows about it. You can imagine what an event that crash was in a small place like this. I'm sorry...' She broke off and put a hand on his arm. 'I do apologise. I'm talking as though it was some kind of circus. For you it was a tragedy, of course.'

'It's perfectly all right,' he said. This woman couldn't upset him, whatever she said. She was a person whose expression radiated a natural sympathy for others. She was curious about him, clearly, but without even a hint of nosiness. 'It was a tragedy for my mother,' Chris went on, 'But I never knew my father. In fact I'm only beginning to get the details now. I want to know what happened, as far as I can.'

'You need to speak to Ben,' the woman said.

'Ben?'

She started to reply, then had another thought. 'Look - would you two like a cup of tea?'

'Well...we don't want to be a nuisance,' Chris began, but Melanie forestalled him.

'We'd love one,' she said.

That settled it. The woman went off to a kitchen somewhere and came back a few minutes later with tea and biscuits. The three of them sat round a small coffee table in the office reception.

'It was a long time ago, that accident,' the woman said, 'But I still have a pretty clear picture of what happened. I was in the village at the time. When the crash occurred it was late afternoon. The plane came down on the West side of Potton Wood, where the water tower is. It just cleared the farmhouse and they say it might have managed a crash landing on the fields, but one wing hit the edge of the wood. It slewed round and ploughed into the trees.' She gave Chris a look that was still full of concern. 'You didn't know any of this?'

'Nothing,' he said. 'But do go on, please. I really want to know.'

'I don't know if you can still tell where the plane hit the wood,' she went on. 'To be honest, I haven't walked near that side for ages. For years after it happened there were clear signs of the accident, but...trees have a way of reclaiming their territory.'

Chris looked out of the window towards the wood, visible in the distance. 'We'll go and have a look after this.'

'When it crashed,' she said, 'Several men from the village ran across to the place.' She gave that anxious look again, worried how Chris would take the information. 'I'm sorry to say that not all of them stayed. The plane was on fire and there was a rumour that bombs were on board.'

'But it was a training flight.'

She nodded. 'I know it doesn't make sense now, but in the

heat of the moment...anyway, two people did stay to try and help. One of them was Mr Taylor, who worked at this office - that's how I know a bit about it. Mr Taylor died two years ago. The other one was Ben, the man I mentioned. He was a farm worker - still is, as far as I know. He and Mr Taylor actually went into the plane and dragged one of the airmen out. Ben was quite badly burnt himself in the process. They tried...' She fell silent, and he sensed there was something else; something she didn't want him to hear.

'Yes?' He leaned forward in his seat.

'It's...not very nice, I'm afraid.'

'Please.'

'Are you sure? Well, they tried to get other airmen out. I don't know if one of them was your father - I really don't. The flames were too fierce. As I say, Ben got badly burnt as it was.' She was quiet for a moment, and then went on. 'As it happens, this building was where they brought the injured man. Mr Taylor came back for his car and brought him here. I didn't work here then, I'm glad to say, because he said the man was very badly burnt. It wasn't a pretty sight.'

'Do you know who that man was?' Chris asked.

'I don't remember the name, but it was one of the Australians.'

'And do you happen to know if he survived?'

'I'm not sure about that. He was taken to the air base hospital at Duxford - in a bad way, but still alive. At least, well enough to be flown back to Australia. We didn't hear any more about him after that.'

They finished their cups of tea and thanked her. 'Leave your address,' said the woman as they got up to leave. 'I'll make some enquiries about Ben. I'm sure I can track him down. Everyone knows everything in a place like this. If you come this way again call in and have a talk to him. There's a lot he could tell - though I must warn you it may make painful hearing.'

Chris thanked her again. She had shed light on a scene concealed from his family for two decades. They went outside and unlocked the church. The building was tiny, and could have provided seating for thirty people at most. Given the limited nature of Cockayne Hatley's population that was probably enough for any occasion likely to arise. The woman had said the church was served every other Sunday by a priest based at a nearby town, so presumably the village mustered some sort of congregation on these occasions. With no faith of his own Chris found it extraordinary that churches were built at all in such remote locations.

Melanie had a good look round the interior, but Chris scarcely gave it a glance. He'd never shared her enthusiasm for the arcane severities of church architecture, and the building could tell him nothing about his father. They locked up and returned the key. Melanie ambled towards the car, but Chris was gazing in the direction of the trees, which formed a dark streak on the horizon. 'I want to have a look at the wood,' he said.

She gave it a dubious look. 'What are you hoping to find there?' she said.

'I don't know. It's just...where it happened.'

'It?'

'The crash, Melanie. It's where my father died.'

He was conscious that she was not enjoying the trip. It had been a mistake, perhaps, to bring someone not directly involved with the accident. For him every step, every detail of the landscape, was important for the light it cast on the past. He was tense with nervous excitement. It was natural that Melanie didn't see it in the same way.

Then she relented, grabbing his arm and striding off in the direction of the car. 'Come on, then. Let's get it over with,' she said, with a gurgling outburst of the laughter that he always found irresistible.

They returned down the approach road, then turned at right angles into another rough track alongside the wood and the water tower. Not far down it was a break in the ploughed field that fronted the trees. A small lane was the obvious route to get in amongst them. Chris parked the car and they set off down it on foot. If the woman in the office had been right this was roughly the approach taken, inadvertently, by the Lancaster. A hundred yards behind them was the farm-house, which the aircraft had only just cleared.

No-one else was in sight and he guessed that the path was rarely used. The ground was rough and very muddy in places, necessitating small diversions. They made slowish progress. Melanie wore a reasonably sensible pair of shoes, but she cursed more than once as her heels sank into thick mud. Chris paid her less attention than he would normally have done. He was in a strange mood, feeling a sudden, strong sense of nearness to his father. Knowing that the accident had occurred twenty years earlier seemed not to matter. It had happened here, amongst these trees. Apart from Edmonton's parish church, this was the only place where both he and his father had been present. Bur *where*, exactly? He scanned the side of the wood without discerning where an aircraft might have ploughed in decades before.

They went over a stile. The path widened, where a broad swathe had been cut through the centre of the wood. He turned right onto a small footpath leading into the trees, behind the water tower. The wind dropped immediately under their cover, so that it suddenly seemed quite warm.

'What now?' said Melanie.

'Don't know, really. Thought we could just walk about here. See what we could see.'

'I've got a better idea,' she said. She took his arm, and led him off the path a little deeper into the forest. There she stopped, rested her back against the broad trunk of a tree, and pulled him towards her. He felt her lips, and smelt her perfume.

'That's better,' she said.

He gave her a hug and started to move away, but she pulled him closer.

'He thinks he can get away,' she murmured. 'He's here on false pretences.'

She pulled his face against hers again, and kissed him deeply. The sensation of it, so familiar, seemed to be happening to someone else. For once in his life kissing Melanie was not what he wanted to do; the time, the place, the mood, all wrong. He turned his head aside and heard her breathing hard in his ear in the silence of the wood. Before he realised what was happening she'd taken his hand and pulled it down between the tops of her thighs. Her free hand was fumbling with the zip of his jeans.

'No,' he said, pulling back sharply, catching a glimpse of her dress up round her waist and her bare flesh pressed against the bark of the trunk. 'Not now. No, Melanie.' He hesitated, unable to find the right words, but also feeling that he shouldn't need to explain.

She was furious. 'Oh, sorry, I'm sure,' she said, moving aside so that her dress fell back into place. She started back up the path in the direction they'd come from, stepping out furiously. He stood there for a moment, longing to plunge further into the wood, then turned to follow her. 'I just thought - don't waste an opportunity,' she threw over her shoulder. 'We get so few.'

'Yes, but...' He was genuinely astonished that their thoughts could have run along such different lines on such a day. Where was the rapport he thought they'd built up? They were like strangers.

She hurled another comment over her retreating back. 'It's not sacred by any chance, is it - this wood?'

'I'm sorry. Let's go back to the car.'

'Yes, let's.'

She scrambled back to the path and retraced her steps, while he followed a short distance behind. He caught her up half way along the approach path and they walked back to the car in silence. Her face had an expression he'd come across a few times before. When that happened it was best to say nothing.

They climbed back into the car and drove away. On Chris's left, the dark face of the wood stared blankly back, secretive, unfriendly. He found himself beginning to dislike it.

~ Eleven ~

June 1964

Chris had learnt a lot on the visit to Potton Wood, but the trip left a sour taste in his mouth. The incident with Melanie was worse than a flaming row. They'd both been quiet all the way back, and when he dropped her off neither of them tried to fix another meeting. He felt very alone. If anything the visit served to confirm that, on this matter, he *was* alone; he couldn't expect anyone else to share his visit to this remote corner of England, his morbid interest in the events of twenty years back, his groping for personal identity. Even before he'd reached home he resolved to go to the wood again, and this time to go on his own. He would linger wherever he wanted to linger and walk amongst the trees; absorb the atmosphere of the place. It was a venture that demanded solitude.

There was one other person who had a stake in the affair and the next morning at breakfast, when Reg had gone off to work, he told his mother about the visit. He'd thought hard about this and felt she should at least have the chance to know what he was doing. She could ask for more details if she wanted to, or leave it alone. The moment he told her he knew that she was interested. Of course she was a woman, and therefore curious about most things, but there was more to it than that. Whether her twenty-year silence on the subject of Gregson's death meant that she'd also repressed all thoughts of her former lover was impossible for Chris to tell. But telling him about the accident had clearly opened his mother up to the possibility of further disclosures. She seemed more relaxed about the subject than he'd imagined. Even so, the threat of her husband's disapproval still weighed heavily.

'Best not to mention any of this to Reg,' she said. 'It's bound to be painful for him.'

'Is it?' Chris wasn't good at penetrating Reg's thought processes.

'Think about it,' she told him. 'I've only been close to two men in my life - your father and Reg. Your father was an airman. Terribly romantic that, Chris, dying young. Reg was a civilian during the war. Not his fault - he was in a reserved occupation. But those things mattered at the time.'

'Does Reg know I'm looking into things?' Chris asked.

'I haven't told him.'

'Nor have I.'

She shrugged. 'I don't really see the point in bothering him with it. He's so busy.'

Chris smiled to himself. She'd gone off at a tangent there, not for the first time in her life. But it was very clear how much her thoughts were on Potton wood. Her expression was far away; twenty years away, perhaps. 'Is it a nice place?' she asked.

'I think it is. It's beautiful. Lonely, though. Why don't you come with me, next time I visit?'

She looked up quickly. 'Oh I don't think so. No...'

'Why don't you?'

'I couldn't.'

'Well, if you change your mind.'

'No.' She shook her head vigorously enough to rule out a 'yes' for good. 'What did Melanie think of it?'

'Not much.' Without going into detail, he told her they'd had a misunderstanding. 'I don't really know what happened,' he said. 'We get on so well usually.'

'Do you?' Susan was looking at him closely.

'Well, yes...don't you think so?'

'I can't say.' She gave a gnomic smile. 'Don't worry - you'll know all right when it's the one.'

'Will I, though? Did *you* know, Mum?'

Chris had spoken without thinking, and as soon as the question was out he regretted its foolishness. His mother turned away, embarrassed. It took him a moment to realise that the colour rising in her sallow features was a blush; he'd never seen that happen before.

'Wouldn't you like to know,' she said, with an attempt at lightness which in no way deceived.

As far as Chris knew she had never in their twenty years together told him a lie; not revealing the story of Gregson's death being the nearest she had come to it. Her reaction to his thoughtless question confirmed Chris's worst suspicions: that she was unhappy in a marriage to a man she didn't love; that she had 'made the best' of things for her son's sake. He wished he hadn't asked, because knowing she was unhappy made him unhappy too.

Over the next few weeks it was hard to get thoughts of

Potton Wood out of his head. Images of the dark sweep of trees against the flat countryside were his constant companions. In quiet moments even the sound of the wind came to haunt him. He longed to return, but before that he wanted to know more about the accident, and in particular how the aircraft had gone into the trees. He made further enquiries at the nearest public library - Chris was beginning to discover how useful libraries could be - and was given the addresses of several collections of aerial photos. The most promising of these turned out to be the photographic library of the National Monuments Record at Swindon, described as 'the most extensive air photographs library in the country'. They had three million items in all, the bulk of them from the RAF Ordnance Survey.

A short correspondence with this organisation (not to mention payment of another fee) resulted, a few weeks later, in his receiving some photographs of Potton Wood and the surrounding countryside. On two of these the entry point of the Lancaster into the wood was clearly depicted, albeit on pictures taken some 15 years after the event. It didn't guarantee the signs were still there, of course; but if he could align the gash at the edge of the wood with the water tower - a useful landmark - that should help to locate the spot once he got back to Cockayne Hatley. Finding the precise location of the accident was becoming important to him. There were no practical gains to be derived from it; he just wanted to know.

May had turned into June before Chris was ready to revisit the wood. He planned to do it on the first Sunday of the month, and when he woke that morning was pleased to see sunlight coming through the bedroom window. Intending an early start he got up - as he thought - before the rest of the household, only to find his sister Alison already at the breakfast table.

'It's a miracle,' she said, as the eyebrows went up in her pale face. 'Up before nine on a Sunday morning.'

'A double miracle,' Chris responded in kind, indicating that she was also present at this unusual hour. He explained the reason for his unaccustomed early rising.

'This is just a thought,' she said, after a while, 'But if you'd like some company there, I could come with you.'

He looked at her. After the fiasco with Melanie he'd visualised taking the trip alone, but now Alison had spoken it seemed entirely right that she should accompany him.

'No, it's all right,' she said quickly. 'I'm sure you'd feel better alone, this time...'

'I wouldn't.' He put a hand on her shoulder. 'It would be really nice if you could come. In fact I'd love you to come.'

She fixed him in the gaze of her enormous green eyes. 'Well that's that, then. Count me in.'

They set off soon after nine-thirty. He knew the way this time, and made very good progress. The roads were empty and there were few people about, though on the lead-in to Royston they passed a group of Hari-Krishna disciples cavorting on the pavement in their exotic costumes. He told Alison all he'd learnt so far about the accident at Potton Wood. Once they reached the road to Cockayne Hatley the open landscape began to re-exert its pull on him.

Alison seemed to feel it too. 'What a lovely spot,' she said.

'Yes. It looks different in the sunlight. Not better, just different.'

The sense of isolation was what he'd most remembered about the location; but when they drew up at St John's church there were several vehicles parked on the approach road.

'Of course - it's a Sunday,' he said. 'This must be one of the fortnightly services. The estate lady talked about them.'

They left the car and walked round to the front of the church. Sunlight fell on the deep green of the yew trees, and the sound of organ music came from the open door of the building. A handful of voices were groaning in worship. They turned to gaze at the sweep of countryside. There was really no need to tell Alison where Potton Wood was, but Chris raised an arm and pointed to the forest belt on the horizon, beyond the ploughed fields. The rural scene, not much changed in decades, he imagined, was utterly remote from Hari Krishna disciples, rock stars, models, mini-skirts, and all the paraphernalia of the 'swinging sixties' depicted in the morning's papers.

They had evidently arrived at the moment that the church

service ended, for the congregation of St John's now spilled out into the churchyard; all seven of them. They were followed by the priest, in cassock and surplice, a lean looking man in his middle forties. He made straight for Chris and Alison.

'You've just missed the service,' he said without introduction. 'A pity. It's not as if we were full up.'

Chris grinned. 'Actually, we didn't come for that. We're just here by chance.' He introduced Alison and explained briefly why they had come.

He could tell immediately that the priest was interested. 'So that's it,' the man said. 'I've heard all about that tragedy, though of course I wasn't around at the time.'

'It seems to be pretty common knowledge around here,' Chris said.

'I should think so.' The priest said goodbye to a decrepit-looking couple who were dragging themselves towards the car park. 'I'm a bit of a local historian myself,' he went on, 'And also...well, to be honest, I'm potty about aircraft. It's a bit of a bug. Don't know what I'm doing in this garb, really. I'd give anything to be up there.'

All three of them looked up at the sky where, twenty years earlier, it would not have been unusual for a violent dog-fight to be disturbing the peace of the morning. The priest wouldn't have looked out of place in flying gear, Chris reflected. The man had an authoritative, muscular quality that was unusual in a man of the cloth. His expression was sympathetic but completely without softness.

'Look,' the priest said, 'My name's David Threlfall. I'd be very interested to know if you find out any more about your father's accident. I'm like quite a few people round here - fascinated by flying and everything to do with it. You never know - if I can be of help any time, get in touch.' He reached into the cassock and drew out his card, which gave an address in Biggleswade. 'Don't hesitate. I'd love to talk about it.'

Chris thanked him, and as he and Alison turned to leave the vicar had another thought.

'Before you go, have a look at our monument.' He pointed

into the churchyard, at the largest grave, which even at a distance could be seen to have a rather florid headstone. 'I thought at first that's what you were here to see - Margaret Henley's grave. It's the usual reason outsiders visit us.

'Henley?'

'She was supposed to be the inspiration for the name of 'Wendy' in Peter Pan,' the priest went on. 'Barrie was a friend of her father's. Apparently she used to call the author 'fwendy'. So, Fwendy became Wendy. That's what they say, anyway. It's worth a look.'

They said goodbye and walked across to the grave, which had by far the most imposing headstone amongst the 30 or so in the churchyard. It was decorated in an unusual style, vaguely familiar to Chris.

'Doesn't this sort of artwork have a name?' he said.

Alison raised an eyebrow. 'I think they call it *art nouveau*,' she said, 'But don't quote me on that.' He couldn't help comparing her unassuming response with Melanie's approach a few weeks earlier, on the subject of church architecture.

The two of them stared at the inscription to Margaret Henley. The poor girl had not lived beyond the age of five, yet people came out to this remote spot to see her grave.

'Sad,' Alison said.

Chris looked across at his step-sister, standing there in no hurry to move on, her pale features stilled in contemplation.

'You could put a stone up here youself,' she said, almost to herself, 'In memory of your father. To all those who died. A monument to the crew of the Lancaster.'

The words fell quietly upon the empty churchyard. Chris didn't say anything in response, and didn't feel the need to. They both knew it was a good suggestion. The idea began to take shape then and there amongst the desiccated tombstones of the churchyard.

'Potton Wood?' Chris said eventually.

She nodded. 'Shall we walk?'

Another good suggestion, Chris thought. As often before, Alison seemed to know what he was thinking almost before he knew it himself. Better to walk the quarter mile to Potton Wood than disturb the peacefulness of the moment by climbing in and out of a car. They set off together down the road. The tiny congregation of St John's church had already evaporated, and the place was once again bereft of people. They walked together past the water tower and down the approach road to the wood. The surface water, so plentiful on his last visit, had evaporated during the spell of good weather, leaving hard, dried mud underfoot. Spring flowers were out and some bees cruised dozily amongst them. As he walked, Chris scanned the face of the wood. He had the aerial pictures from Swindon in his pocket, but found it difficult to match up the photographic evidence - the clear gash shown in the trees at the edge - with the blank face of the wood itself.

Reaching the trees, they turned onto the path just inside them. He wanted to use the water tower as a landmark to try and identify the aircraft's point of entry. Alison was ahead of him on the narrow path, and in a moment she stopped.

'It's here,' she said.

Chris followed the direction of his sister's gaze. There was no doubt about it. The disturbance to the perimeter of the wood, unclear to anyone outside looking in, was immediately obvious once they'd moved amongst the trees themselves. The scarred and broken tree-trunks along a fifty-yard stretch were only partially restored by the renewal process, which had already spanned two decades since the accident. They stood side by side, both striving to make a link between past and present. In the quietness that enfolded them it was hard to conjure an impression of the violent collision that had caused such damage. Chris tried to imagine the clamour of the Lancaster's engines as the aircraft careered across fields and into the trees; the tearing of wood and crash of falling branches; the crackle of flames, the thing that airmen feared most of all; then the cries of wounded men trapped in the wreckage.

As a city dweller Chris was unused to the curious intimacy of woods. He went from tree to tree, touching the scarred trunks, preoccupied with his thoughts. Looking up, he saw Alison some yards further in, meandering across ground strewn with the forest debris. She stopped to lean her plump body comfortably against the trunk of a tree. He was again struck by her composure compared to Melanie's obvious discomfiture in the same surroundings six weeks earlier. Alison was someone who accepted her environment without resistance, taking pleasure from ordinary things. He thought how fortunate he'd been in his step-sister. Their years together had rendered her company so congenial to him, yet he took it for granted.

'Chris.'

Alison was kneeling on the forest floor. As he approached, she held something up to him.

'What's this?' she said.

She was grasping a small fragment of aluminium, roughly two inches square, with serrated edges. He had no hesitation in naming its provenance.

'It's a piece of fuselage,' he said.

She scrambled to her feet. 'I don't know enough about these things,' she went on. 'What happens when a plane crashes? There must be pieces everywhere.'

'It'd make a damn big crater in the ground. They'd tow away the main part of the plane, then fill in the crater. But as the aircraft tears through the trees, stuff will fly off in all directions. There'll be lots of bits around here. D'you know, I hadn't thought of that.'

He stood there shifting the piece of fuselage from hand to hand. He was accustomed to handling model components representing parts of planes, but this was the first time he'd actually had a piece of the real thing in his grasp. He lingered for some while, deeply preoccupied. His sister came up behind and rested her head on his shoulders. Their place within the trees was absolutely silent, shielded from the wind that strafed the open countryside. It was a kind of peace, being there. He thought: there are worse places to die than this.

~ Twelve ~

June - September 1964

After his second visit to Potton Wood Chris found events gathering pace at an alarming rate. The catalyst was Alison's suggestion of a memorial stone for the Cockayne Hatley churchyard, an idea that grew in appeal the more he thought about it. It answered his need for some tangible sign of John Gregson's existence, and would be at least something to celebrate a man who had melted into thin air; whose funeral had not even been attended by his pregnant lover. A stone in the churchyard, facing the sweep of open land towards Potton Wood, would be a permanent reminder of his father's life and death, and of those who had died with him.

First he had to clear the idea with the one other person who was intimately involved. One, or possibly two. The situation as it affected Susan and Reg was undeniably delicate. He broached the subject one evening, sitting in the kitchen with his mother and Alison.

'Mum - Alison's had the idea of a memorial stone at Cockayne Hatley. Something to commemorate the men who died there. What do you reckon?'

'Goodness!' Susan put her head in her hands for a moment, elbows on the kitchen table. When she raised her head, Chris thought he saw his mother's expression pass through several phases: her debt of guilt to him, her loyalty to Reg, and her own private feelings about the matter, whatever they were.

'I think it's a good idea,' she said at last. 'Good for you, because he's been such an absence from your life - and that's my fault, by the way. Good for me, too,' she continued, with a touch of her old gay abandon. 'He just...vanished without trace, all those years ago. It would be nice to have a reminder. It wouldn't do any harm.'

Chris knew that the last remark referred to Reg.

Alison, with her usual gift for doing the right thing, turned the conversation to practical matters. 'But do you know *how* to put up a memorial stone? It's not like a gravestone, is it?'

'I've absolutely no idea,' Chris said, 'But I'll find out. Meeting the priest up at St John's should be a help. I've got his card.'

'It won't be cheap,' said Susan. 'A good stone mason will set you back a bit.'

'I've got a couple of thousand in that savings account - thanks to you and Reg. I'd like to spend some of it that way.'

'Chris...' She was looking tentative. 'If this does go ahead, will you let me go halves with you? I've some money of my own. I'd like to chip in.'

'Blimey, Mum.' He was taken aback, but shouldn't have been; she'd always been one for springing surprises. 'I'd really like that,' he said at length, 'If you're sure it's all right...'

'Of course it's all right. Don't worry.'

It may have been 'all right', but she still jumped slightly as Reg came into the kitchen through the back door. His entrance jarred the intimate, almost collusive atmosphere. He seemed to fill the small room with his thick-set figure. Susan broke the uncomfortable pause.

'We were talking about a memorial, Reg, at the place where Chris's father was killed. A stone in the churchyard for all the crew. It seems like a good idea. Don't you think so?'

Later Chris came to believe that it was then Reg felt the first tremor of future events. He stood four-square, breathing rather heavily, facing the three members of his family. He reminded Chris of a hunted animal at bay.

'Isn't it best to leave the past alone?' he said at length.

'It's just a memorial,' Susan said. 'It won't do any harm. It would be good for Chris to have something - to show what happened.'

'I can see that,' Reg said, head down. His face wore a strange expression, like a man holding back tears. He moved to go upstairs, then turned back at the kitchen door. 'Well, whatever you decide.' When he'd gone Susan exchanged a glance with Alison, but nothing more was said.

Later that week Chris called on his father's aunt again, and explained what he had in mind. She was enthusiastic. To his surprise she also talked about money.

'I'm an old woman with money in the bank and nothing to spend it on,' she said. 'Will you let me make a contribution? I'd like nothing better. Talk to your mother. If you both agree, perhaps we could split it three ways.'

Suddenly Chris felt everyone was thrusting cash at him; at this rate, he thought, I'll come out of it with a profit.

Next he wrote to David Threlfall, the vicar at the Cockayne Hatley church. Chris reminded him they'd met the previous Sunday and said his sister had suggested a memorial stone to the men of the crashed Lancaster. Did the vicar feel something of this kind would be possible? And if so what steps should now be taken? Threlfall replied almost immediately, and raised a further intriguing possibility.

Dear Mr Nash

It was good to hear from you so soon after our brief talk outside St John's. Your suggestion of a memorial stone to the crew who died in the Lancaster is immediately appealing. As the parish priest here I would certainly support it. Since the stone would be on sacred ground I should need to obtain permission from the Church of England authorities, but I foresee no difficulties about this. If you are sure that you want to go ahead, I will make enquiries immediately.

I wonder if I may put another suggestion to you. If a stone is to be put into the ground I expect you would want to make a special day of it, and bring a party with you for its inauguration. If that day were to be a Sunday, I should be very happy to hold a small service at the church, for yourselves and for any local people who wanted to attend. As you know, there are still several people in the area who were involved in the rescue at the time, and I am sure they would want to be there.

Perhaps you could telephone to give your thoughts about this, and - if you like the idea - to talk about a possible date. By the way, do you know the date of the accident itself? I believe it happened during the Summer. I suppose it might just happen to coincide with a Sunday inauguration date. I look forward to hearing from you.

Yours sincerely, David Threlfall.

Here is a man accustomed to involving himself in other people's problems, Chris thought. He went to the calendar and turned up the September entries, and there it was. September 18 was the twenty-first anniversary of his father's death and it coincided with a Sunday. If he'd believed in omens this would surely have been one.

He telephoned David Threlfall the same day and said that the dates fitted.

'I had a feeling about that,' the vicar said. 'These things are sometimes looked after for us.' Threlfall was not finished with the helpful information. 'You know, some of the men who knew your father - and the rest of the crew - would be interested in this event,' he said. 'Some might even want to come to it.'

'That's true, but I don't have any names,' Chris said, 'Except for one friend of my father's, who my mother once met - and I don't even know where he is. He may not be alive.'

'That was always a problem with the bombing crews,' Threlfall said soberly. 'Have you heard of something called *Airmail*?'

Chris hadn't.

'It's an old soldiers' magazine. Old airmen, in this case. I think it bills itself as 'the journal of the RAF Association'. It's really a way of keeping former fliers in touch. Absolutely packed with little items harking back to the war. The thing is read with manic intensity by men who flew in those awful days, and even by some sad characters who didn't - like me, for instance. I'm going to send you an old copy in today's post.'

'You mean - you think they'd publish an item by me?'

'I'm sure they would.'

'I suppose someone might be interested.'

'Interested? You'd be amazed. Those days are never out of their heads. They don't talk about it much, but they think it. Not surprising, I suppose. Ghastly as the war was, its participants led a heightened form of existence. We can't even guess at it, with our nanny state - everything taken care of.'

'I suppose not.'

The vicar laughed, at himself if anything. 'Sorry to bang on. The welfare state's a bit of an obsession with me. Ah...one possible problem. *Airmail* only does a few issues a year. You could be unlucky on submission dates.'

Threlfall's promised copy of *Airmail* arrived the next morning. The thing was cheaply put together but contained a mass of information about flying. A large 'Help' section was stacked with items from former fliers, most of them requesting information: a man writing a book about 617 squadron wanted reminiscences; a former pilot hoped to contact his flight engineer; another pilot wanted to hear from his old rear gunner, who had bailed out over Berlin twenty-two years earlier.

Chris found the editor's telephone number and gave him a ring. The submissions deadline fell very conveniently; at the end of June for publication in mid-July. He compiled a short piece about his plans for a memorial stone and a service on 18th September, and gave an address and telephone number for anyone who wanted more information. He posted it off with a silent prayer that all his plans matured; if not, he would be left looking very silly. Events seemed to be generating themselves at a pace beyond his control. After all, he was a 21-year old student who'd never organised anything more taxing than a skittles evening at the local pub.

In the same post as the copy of *Airmail* was a note from the lady at the Cockayne Hatley estate office. She gave the name of the Australian airman who'd been pulled alive from the burning Lancaster: Peter Freshwater. She also gave an address and telephone number for 'Ben', the farm labourer who'd helped to pull Freshwater out. Chris had forgotten all about her promise to write. She apologised for the delay and said she'd had difficulty locating the man, finally tracking him down to a Cambridgeshire village quite near to Cockayne Hatley.

Chris sat straight down and wrote Ben a letter too, describing the plans for a memorial and inviting him to attend the service. He had a short reply a week later, in a hand which was obviously not used to writing.

Dear Mr Nash
Thank you for your letter. Sorry I could not help you're father too. Stone is good idea. I will try to come but not feeling very well nowdays. Yours, Ben Silver.

Meanwhile Chris had embarked on arrangements for getting the stone cut. Melanie was a help there. Chris had only seen her twice in the preceding weeks, but he'd asked her to keep the 18th of September free. When he explained about the memorial stone she offered to make enquiries through her design lecturers at college. Two days later she phoned through an address: an outfit called 'Memorials by Artists', based in Suffolk. Chris wrote to them describing what he wanted, and got a quick reply suggesting a couple of engravers they thought might be suitable, and who were also available. Enclosed were some photographs of their recent work.

He took these round to Melanie. She was impressed (and so was he) by the work of a man called Derry Holmes, who lived not far away in Potters Bar. Chris drove over to see him one evening. He'd imagined stone cutters to be old and somewhat inarticulate, but Derry Holmes was quite different: in his middle thirties, indisputably middle-class, affable and hospitable, though with a slightly distracted air. He wore a jacket without a collar - a distinct novelty. Over a cup of tea Chris described the remote churchyard at Cockayne Hatley, and the way it was exposed to the wind sweeping across open countryside.

'In those conditions we might consider slate,' the stone-cutter said. 'It's hard enough to withstand anything.'

'Slate? I really wanted a smoother substance.'

Holmes grinned. 'You're thinking of roof slates. Slate can be as smooth as you like. It's a lovely material. I'll show you some examples in a minute. What sort of wording do you want?'

Chris had given some thought to this but by no means reached a conclusion. He described in detail all he knew about the accident. 'I was thinking the stone should identify the aircraft and where it crashed,' Chris said, 'And the date. And then the names of the crew.'

'There are two constraints on wording,' Holmes said. 'The amount of lettering you can get onto the stone, and...well, not to put too fine a point on it, the cost.'

'If we're going to do this, I want to do it properly,' Chris said. 'I do have one problem about names. I know about those who were killed in the accident, but there was also one survivor. At least, they think he survived. No-one's quite sure.'

'I see.' Despite the laid-back air, the engraver seemed pretty quick to grasp his client's concerns. 'Pity to leave him out.'

'I think so too. It just makes a difficulty with the wording.'

'Look Chris - you'll first need to decide if you'd like me to go ahead with this work...'

'No need for more thought on that.' Chris had taken to Holmes, as he had to his work. 'I'd like to go ahead - as long as I can manage the price.'

'Then you go home and work out some alternative forms of wording. I'll work on the shape of the stone, and the disposition of lettering on it. Between us we'll get a fix on cost - but it's not likely to exceed a thousand pounds.'

'Then let's do it.'

'Splendid. I'll also drive out to Cockayne Hatley and have a look. That always helps.'

In the next week Chris covered sheets of paper with different forms of wording. He thought a lot about Peter Freshwater, the man who had survived the immediate crash, and in all probability was alive somewhere in Australia at that moment. It would be good to have Freshwater's name on the stone; he was the one positive feature of the story. At the back of Chris's mind was the letter he'd had from Ben Silver, the farm labourer who had risked his own life to go in and pull Freshwater clear. First and foremost the accident had been a tragedy for the crew, of course, but it had also been important to local people. The woman in the office had made that clear. After many attempts, he came up with a form of words that he was reasonably happy with:

For the crew of Lancaster 372 which crashed in Potton Wood 18 September 1944

Saved with the help of local people: F/O P FRESHWATER RAAF

Killed on duty:
(and here he added the names and ranks of the other five

crew members, including his father)

He posted this off to Derry Holmes, and had a call from him the next day.

'The wording's OK,' Holmes said. 'I can get that on all right. Look, I've had an idea about the stone. I'd like to know what you think. Suppose we do it in the form of a wing? The wing of an aircraft?'

Chris didn't even need to hesitate. 'That's absolutely brilliant,' he said. 'Of course. *Of course.* How did you think of it?'

'Pure genius,' the engraver said. 'It just came to me, like all the best ideas. Glad you like it. I'll get your words down onto a mock-up wing now, and send you the results.'

In short time his suggested layout came back through the post. Chris showed it to his mother and to Marjorie Gregson. They were in favour, and he asked Holmes to go ahead with an estimate, which came out at just below the predicted thousand.

Chris noticed a change in his life-style around this time. Over the Summer, arrangements for the Cockayne Hatley ceremony took up a surprising amount of his time. What with that and the daily shifts at the Hammer and Pincers he found he was doing very little work on the Liberator model in his bedroom. What was more, he felt no real desire to make time for the old modelling activity. Recent events had supplanted it. He had the curious sense of a make-believe world being brought to life.

From mid-July on there was more information to cast light on what had happened during the the war. The summer edition of *Airmail* was out, with his own announcement in it, and almost immediately he began to receive letters from former airmen who had known his father. There was a highly complimentary one from his squadron leader in 1943, and another from a man who had roomed with him when they were based near Miami (and who claimed his father owed him a pint of beer). One of Gregson's former navigators wrote, enclosing his unpublished memoirs – *Where are we now, skip?* - in which the pilot featured several times. There were quite a few more. The priest at St John's had clearly been right when he said *Airmail* was widely read amongst former airmen. Even better, at least two of the respondents reported that they would be coming to the ceremony: a man who had shared basic training with his father; and someone else called Freddy Mitchell, who described himself as a close friend of John Gregson, who had been his flight engineer on the last 30 missions over enemy territory.

As the day of the ceremony approached, Chris began to get nervous. Really nervous. He'd never done anything like this before and was conscious of how many things could go wrong - not least, a stormy day which could ruin the ceremony out in the churchyard. Fortunately the vicar at St John's had been extraordinarily helpful throughout the planning stage, and was clearly a man used to organising events. All the same Chris went over and over what needed to be done, trying to make sure the day would go smoothly.

Three days before the 18th he sat down and listed the people who were likely to be there. He'd originally envisaged a small group of half a dozen, but that seemed a very long time ago. The numbers had swelled considerably. Of his immediate family, Susan and Reg were going, and Alison. (Brother Gary had turned it down, he was relieved to hear.) Then Melanie, of course, and Marjorie Gregson had said she 'would not miss it for worlds'. Derry Holmes, the stone carver would be there, actually putting the stone into the ground. And the lady from the estate office. There were also several people he'd not met: Christian Smythe, who had done the original research at Hendon museum, and asked to be included; the two former airmen; and - if he was well enough to turn up - Ben Silver, who'd pulled Freshwater from the wreckage. To these would be added the priest, the usual congregation of St John's, and any of the local population who were interested. Quite a crowd.

Minus one. When Chris got back from a late shift at the Hammer and Pincers one evening Susan met him in the kitchen.

'You had a call from Melanie about Sunday,' she said. 'She's not coming. She says she's sorry.'

He could see his mother watching anxiously but Chris's reaction was a surprise, even to himself. There was a moment of disappointment, but it lasted no longer than that. He'd known it was over with Melanie ever since that incident in Potton Wood. Her message was merely a delayed recognition of something they both acknowledged. It was sad, but he needed to move on - and so did she.

'I expect you'll ring her,' his mother said.

'I will, Mum, to say goodbye. I don't think we'll be seeing each other again.'

'I'm sorry.'

'Never mind,' he said. 'It was good while it lasted. The important thing now is to give my father a proper send off.'

~ Thirteen ~

18 September 1964

The forecast for the 18th was fine, and when Chris woke to blue skies he gave a shout of relief. The cry woke his mother and Reg in the next room, and even Alison, further down the corridor. Before breakfast he went out into the garden and stood with his face turned towards the sun. There was a freshness in the air that promised a really nice day.

The family had worked out travel arrangements between them. Susan and Reg had offered to go over to Edmonton to pick up Marjorie Gregson and drive her to Bedfordshire. Chris drove to Cockayne Hatley early, to be around before the other visitors. When he reached St John's church some time after noon David Threlfall was already there preparing for the service. They stood together at the entrance to the church, looking out across fields lit up by sunshine. The scene was tremendously peaceful. To a city dweller like Chris the sky seemed immense; out in the open its 180-degree span always took him by surprise.

'Isn't it beautiful,' said Threlfall, turning reluctantly to go back into his church.

'Is everything OK?' Chris asked.

Threlfall took his arm. 'You're not to worry. It's going to be a lovely occasion. Oh, by the way...' The vicar threw a conspiratorial glance. 'I've lined up a surprise for you.'

'What do you mean?'

'Not another word.' Threlfall winked and hurried away into St John's.

Chris did a circuit round the church and found Derry Holmes already at work in the modest-sized graveyard. The engraver was on his knees before the memorial stone, which lay flat on the ground at the edge of the area designated for graves. Beside the stone was a deep, narrow slit in the turf. Lying flush to the ground as it was, the slate surface looked drab and somewhat unimpressive.

'I won't shake hands,' Derry said, showing palms ingrained with soil. 'And don't worry. This'll look a lot better when it's upright.'

'Why do people keep telling me not to worry?'

'Because you look worried?'

Chris laughed. He *was* worried, dammit. A lot could go wrong. 'When does the stone go into the ground?' he said.

'Ah, that's the easy bit. Thought I'd put it in during the service. Then when people come out afterwards...bingo. A *coup de theatre*.'

'Pardon?'

'It's French. A sudden revelation. A surprise.'

'Oh! I see. It means you'll miss the service, though.'

'I'll catch the end of it. I've a few things to do here first.'

Chris sat on a rock near the church and, with a view of the wood before him, ate some sandwiches from their wrapping of greaseproof paper. After a while the early cars arrived in the drive, and people began drifting across to the churchyard. One of the first was the researcher, Christian Smythe, a man whom Chris had not actually met before. Smythe was in his fifties, enthusiastic and talkative. He seemed as excited about the event as anyone. Chris again sensed the passion that drew some men of Smythe's generation back to the exploits of fliers in the war; the preoccupation, not entirely healthy, with events that had shaped their lives and could not be forgotten.

As two o'clock approached, things began to happen all at

once. Local residents started to walk across from the houses scattered in the village. More cars drew up, almost in convoy, disgorging people - some known to Chris, others not. One vehicle contained his mother, Reg, Alison, and Marjorie Gregson, and he went across to greet them. Alison was as impassive as ever and Miss Gregson looked distinctly pleased to be present, but Susan and Reg both seemed on edge. His mother's pale face had a febrile, nervous expression. Reg looked out of place; he wore a suit that was too heavy for such a warm day, and was clasping and unclasping his hands anxiously. Chris had rarely seen him so lacking in composure. He noticed Alison lean up to kiss her father, seeking to put him at ease.

Chris took hold of Miss Gregson's hands, and thanked her warmly for coming.

'Oh no - I'm absolutely delighted to be here, Chris,' she said. 'And you have to learn to call me Marjorie.'

He showed them where they would be sitting inside the church, then returned outside, looking vainly around for anyone who might be Freddy Mitchell, his father's old flight engineer. He hadn't anticipated the difficulties of identifying people in this melee; the churchyard was alive with movement and colour. He turned at a tug on his sleeve and recognised the lady from the Cockayne Hatley office, standing together with an older man and a young woman.

'Hello again,' she said. 'I want to introduce you to Ben Silver and his daughter. Ben is the man I told you about. He helped to pull one of the airmen from the plane.' She turned to her companions. 'This is Chris Nash. He's organised the memorial stone. His father was one of the pilots killed in the accident.'

The man was in his early sixties, short, with a barrel-chested frame which had once been very powerful, though he now seemed shaky and unwell. He looked uncomfortable in a suit which was too large for him and seemed almost new. His hands, large and rough with the effects of manual work, trembled slightly. Chris thanked him for the letter and for coming to the service.

'Wanted to come,' Silver said, in a thick voice. 'Seems like only yesterday, that plane coming down.' He turned to look in the direction of the wood.

'I've heard what you did,' Chris said. 'Saving one of the men.'

'Wanted to do more,' Silver said indistinctly. He looked away, troubled, it seemed, even at this distance from the event.

David Threlfall was moving about, trying to get people to go in to the church. 'Mr Silver, I would love to talk more about this,' Chris said. 'Do you think we could meet, some time?'

The man looked away again. 'I don't know. Weren't a good sight. There's things you don't want to know, Mr Nash.' Chris held his gaze, and Silver suddenly relented. 'I'll talk to yer, course I will, if'n you're sure you want to hear. Come round after. I don't live no more than three mile away.'

'Are you sure?'

'Course. My daughter'll get you there. Put 'er in your car after the service. Come 'n 'ave some tea with us.'

They had to break off then to join people going into the church. There were still several Chris hadn't met. The vicar seemed anxious to start on time, and was rounding up visitors like a well-trained sheep dog.

'Make a start, Christopher?' he said crisply, looking at his watch.

The tiny church had but two main rows of pews, facing each other, and one of these was taken up by local parishioners. There was some uncertainty amongst the visitors as to who should fill the other. Chris motioned Marjorie Gregson and the three members of his immediate family into it. Reg, sweating in his heavy suit, looked ill at ease, and made as if to move away.

'I'll sit in the places at the back, Susan,' he murmured. 'That makes more sense.'

Susan turned on him. 'Reg, you belong here with me,' she whispered, quite loudly. 'I'm not having you sitting on your own.'

He subsided immediately by her side. It was a novel experience for Chris to see his mother confronting her husband and winning the argument, yet in the past couple of months she'd done it more than once.

The other guests crowded into seats at the back, almost filling the church. Then the vicar began his opening address. 'We have come together today to commemorate those who died in the crash of Lancaster 372 in Potton Wood on 18th September 1944. For some of these men it was a tragic irony that they had survived so many dangers during the war, only to die on a training mission. For others, death came before they had seen active service. We mourn them all. We are delighted to welcome here today Ben Silver, a local man who fearlessly entered the burning plane to help the airmen...'

Threlfall warmed to his theme, putting across the subject in a way that was both delicate and powerful. Chris was the last person to appreciate a priest sermonising in a church service, but there was nothing in the vicar's manner that could conceivably have irritated a non-believer. The man came over as an intellectual, but also as someone who'd experienced life outside his own narrow province; a man who could set the fateful accident in a broader context.

After Threlfall's introduction the congregation sang the hymn 'O God, our help in ages past'. The visitors, swelling the usual congregation, generated an impressive sound; and probably as much volume, Chris thought, as this little church had heard in many a year.

Time, like an ever-rolling stream,
bears all its sons away;
they fly forgotten, as a dream
dies at the opening day.

He looked across at the row of Cockayne Hatley inhabitants in the pew opposite. Time had been unkind to more than one of them. An oldish man, got up in a dark suit with his tie skew-whiff, shook visibly as he clutched the top of the wooden support. A middle-aged woman beside him had a vacant expression on her face, and barely mouthed the words of the hymn.

The vicar was speaking again, looking at his watch. 'Now then...I'd like to interrupt the service and invite you all to come outside for a few minutes. If everything goes to plan - which things rarely do, of course - I hope we can see something that symbolises the theme of this afternoon's service. May I ask you please to move out through the main door.'

There were murmurs of surprise from the pews. Alison leant forward along the row and addressed Chris in a stage whisper.

'What's happening?'

'Don't ask me.'

'But you're the one who's organised all this.'

'He did say just before the service he had a surprise. I don't know, Alison...'

People straggled out, blinking in the strong sunlight. Threlfall led the way to a grassy spot some twenty yards from the church, and was surrounded by an obedient congregation; he looked like a man about to deliver a modern-day version of the sermon on the mount.

But the sound they heard was not that of a human voice. From somewhere nearby - it was hard to tell where, exactly - came a low droning noise, swelling slowly in volume. It might have been a neighbour's lawnmower approaching from afar, or a particularly large bumble bee labouring over some Summer flowers.

Christian Smythe, the researcher, was the first to react. He raised his face like a bloodhound sniffing the air, then began to scan the sky.

'I'd know that sound anywhere,' he cried.

Chris followed his gaze and saw the source of the drone, high in the blue sky. A single word was tossed about between members of the congregation as they craned their necks upwards.

'Spitfire.'

'Spitfire, surely.'

'It's a Spitfire.'

It was a Spitfire all right: a mark XIX, Chris told himself pedantically. To see one flying solo over the English countryside brought a rare mixture of emotions. It was hard to separate the mythology of the famous aircraft from its presence here in the era of jet technology. The Spitfire seemed beautiful, in its way, but also old-fashioned and vulnerable. Impossible now to imagine this fragile flying machine killing and being killed in a hail of bullets, high over fields of grazing cows. Chris dragged his eyes from it for a moment, and saw handkerchiefs coming out all around the congregation, people dabbing furtively at their eyes. His own throat had seized up in a peculiar way. When he looked up again the pilot had begun to dive low over the church; then, as an encore, he executed the celebrated loop-the-loop routine. The old plane managed it easily enough but an air of sadness attached itself to the manoeuvre. It was as though a middle-aged man had laboured to demonstrate some athletic feat which his teenage son could have accomplished with a fraction of the effort.

The Spitfire droned off into the distance, waggling its wings, and no-one moved or spoke until the vicar broke the spell by heading back towards St John's, calling to his flock. As people drifted after him Chris saw a thick-set man in his middle forties step forward to address the group which included his mother.

'Susan? Is it really you?'

Chris could see from the high colouring in her face that his mother was in an emotional state, and she turned to the newcomer now, exclaiming faintly. 'Freddy!'

'Susan. I can't believe it.' The man moved forward awkwardly to shake hands. 'It's been so long.'

The niceties of English manners demanded an introduction to the husband standing beside her, but Susan was clearly not up to it. She stood transfixed, her lips moving but producing no sound, her vocal chords apparently jammed. The church service, the Spitfire, the sight of this man whom she had once known, all these things had released a flood of memories. She had come to the event, husband on arm, in careful control of herself – as she thought – only to find the past sweep over her to devastating effect.

'Reg.' The word came out in an odd little squeak. She stood there gesturing towards her husband until Freddy came to the rescue and introduced himself. He and Reg shook hands cautiously: strangers with the most tenuous of links between them.

Susan recovered up to a point, and managed to introduce the man called Freddy to Marjorie Gregson.

'I believe we've met,' Miss Gregson said. 'At the funeral...?'

Freddy hesitated. 'Yes, of course,' he said. 'I'm sorry.'

'Oh, no need to apologise,' Miss Gregson said. 'I've grown two decades older since then. 'You haven't changed that much, though.'

For a moment it looked as if Freddy would protest at that. Certainly it was hard to imagine his stolid figure in the cockpit of a Lancaster now. But he contented himself with a sigh and a mournful comment: 'What an age ago that seems.'

They were obliged to break off because Threlfall was urging people back into the building.

'Thanks a million for the Spitfire,' Chris said, as he passed the vicar.

Threlfall grinned. 'Glad you liked it. I know someone down at Duxford. Actually, they're only too glad for an excuse to go up in one.'

'It was a wonderful surprise.'

'I wish I'd been up there flying the thing,' Threlfall said with feeling.

Back in the church the remainder of the service passed quickly, and in no time they had reached the final part - the dedication of the memorial. For this Threlfall took the congregation outside again to the same spot, and asked them to turn to face Potton Wood.

'We dedicate this memorial to the memory of Flying Officer Freshwater, Flight Lieutenant Gregson, Flight Lieutenant Turner...'

He read the names of the six men in the doomed aircraft. In the quiet afternoon his voice rolled away across ploughed fields towards the dark, almost sinister line of Potton Wood in the distance. The congregation stood silent.

'They shall not grow old as we that are left grow old. Age shall not weary them, nor the years condemn. At the going down of the sun and in the morning we will remember them.'

'We will remember them,' muttered the flock.

'Almighty and eternal God...'

The vicar launched into his final prayer. Chris felt a hand slipped into his and found Alison at his side. Tears pricked at the back of his eyes. Hearing those lines, with the wood in the background, he felt the loss of his father more strongly than at any time since first seeing the words 'John Gregson' on the birth certificate. With the ceremony almost over the strain of organising the event lifted from his shoulders, and the sense of grief washed over him. How right the words of the prayer were. ' Age shall not weary them, nor the years condemn.' His father's image had scarcely tarnished over the years. The airmen who wrote to him via the note in *Airmail* had stressed Gregson's qualities, not his faults. In Susan's eyes too he was, Chris felt sure, the boyish young war hero. In contrast, the portly figure of Freddy - or for that matter, the battered local parishioners in their pew - was a reminder of what time could bring in its wake.

All that meant less than nothing to Chris now. He yearned for his father to be alive, with all the imperfections and physical depredations of middle age; no hero. He looked across at his mother as she stood amongst the knot of people, holding on to Reg's arm, and wondered how much of this was going through her head.

The service over, people drifted round the side of the church to look at the memorial stone. Derry Holmes stood beside it to semi-attention, like a rather lackadaisical guardsman. The memorial was in place on the very edge of the graveyard, with the inscription facing Potton Wood. Derry had been right about a transformation. The slender stone had taken wing, rising elegantly from the ground. The simple words made moving testimony: 'Saved with the help of local people, F/O P Freshwater; killed on duty...', and the names of the five dead airmen.

'It's beautiful,' Chris told the engraver.

Derry raised both thumbs upwards. 'Said it would be all right, didn't I?'

It was extraordinary to see the churchyard so lively, in contrast to the usual solitary scene. There were groups of people chattering all over the area, local residents mixing with visitors. The area resembled an outdoor cocktail party without food or drink. Susan and Marjorie Gregson were in lively discussion with Freddy Mitchell. Threlfall moved from group to group with a word for everyone.

Chris found it hard to think with so much going on. He was by the memorial stone, looking round for visitors who'd not been unidentified, when he became aware of a stranger standing at his side. The man was in his mid-forties, stocky, with unusually jowly features. It would have been hard not to notice the newcomer because one side of his face was disfigured by the most terrible scars, which could only have been the result of severe burning.

'Are you Chris Nash?' the man asked.

'Yes.'

'It's a beaut of a stone,' he said, and now Chris noticed the strong Australian accent. 'And the names you've got there are spot on. But I have to break the bad news - you're a man and a dog short.'

Chris stared. He was finding it hard to take on board what the man had said. The murmur of conversation continued around them.

'I'm sorry,' the newcomer said, holding out his hand. 'Peter Freshwater.'

Still Chris stared, speechless, until Freshwater pointed to the name at the top of the memorial stone.

'That's me. It's real nice to be included.'

Like most people at times of mental turmoil, Chris fell back on trivialities. 'How did you get here?' he stammered.

'As they say in the movies, I came as soon as I could.' Freshwater laughed. 'Saw your note in *Airmail*. That magazine takes a while to reach Oz. I get it by surface mail.'

Chris had an echo of Freshwater's opening comment banging away at the back of his mind, yet found himself continuing to ask about the man's trip. 'So, you saw it...and then you came across?' he said inanely.

Freshwater shook his head ruefully, so that both sides of his face were visible in short succession. Because of the terrible marks on one side, he had two completely different profiles. 'The crash was kind've a significant bit of my life,' he said. 'I wanted to be here...for this.' He gestured around the churchyard. 'I'd been meaning to come back. It's a funny thing - takes at least twenty years, in my experience, for people to chase up these wartime memories. I saw that edition of *Airmail*, went to see my boss - told him he'd have to do without me for a couple of weeks - and hopped on the first plane I could get. And that'll show you how keen I was to be here. It's the first time I've been on a kite since the accident. I got a bit of a phobia about it.'

He didn't look like a man with phobias. He stood there with his jaw stuck out pugnaciously. Chris couldn't help looking at the left side of his face. 'It's hardly surprising,' he said. 'The phobia, I mean.'

Freshwater fingered his jaw. 'No. Kind've left its mark, didn't it?'

'So how long have you been in England?'

The Australian looked at his watch. 'I'd say about five hours. I got in to Heathrow this morning. Came straight down here. Nearly missed the whole thing. I drifted up right at the end of the service, when the Holy Joe was dedicating the stone.' He hesitated for a moment. 'Look, let me get this right. You're the son of the Lancaster's pilot, right?'

Chris nodded. 'That's right. He wasn't married, but I'm his son just the same.' He pointed to a group on the fringe of the churchyard. 'That's my mother over there - the slim, dark woman.'

There were things Chris was dying to ask him, but they were interrupted by Threlfall, introducing another local man who'd seen the accident when it happened. Then of course Chris had to introduce Freshwater to the vicar, and the two of them spoke for a while. Chris stood by, almost dancing with frustration. As soon as he decently could he waded in and drew Freshwater to one side.

'Look - I'm longing to ask you about something.'

'Yeah, I think you need to,' the Aussie said.

'Could we just get out of the throng for a moment, to talk. Nip into the church, perhaps?'

'Come on, then.'

They stole away from the gathering in the churchyard, which showed no signs of breaking up, and sat side by side in a pew at the back of the church. It was dark, and quiet.

'I'm so glad to meet you, Mr Freshwater,' Chris said.

'I'm Peter.'

'Peter. Look - the first thing you said to me out there - I thought you said "a man and a dog short" - I didn't understand what you meant.'

'I don't blame you. These wartime accidents were a whole mass of confusion, Chris. This one more than most, looks like. When I said you're one name short, I meant there weren't six men on that plane. There were seven.'

Again Chris sat and stared at him. His mouth dropped open slightly, though he was unaware of it. All at once there seemed to be a chill in the nave of the church. 'But...the accident report gave six.'

'That so? I never saw it.'

Chris shook his head almost violently, unable to absorb what the Australian was telling him.

'Let's start from the beginning,' Freshwater said. 'I'm afraid I'm going to be less help than you think, Chris, because I don't remember anything about the flight itself. Can't recall the crash or what followed, thank God. My brain's just shut it out. I gather that's pretty common - there's a medical name for the condition.' He turned in the pew to look Chris directly in the eyes. 'But what happened before the flight I can remember all right, and one thing I do know is that we started off with seven people. One of 'em arrived at the last minute.'

'Are you sure?'

'Sure as I can be.'

'But...why? Who was he?'

'Dunno, mate. He knew your dad. Wanted to go up, for some reason. It happened sometimes. My skipper - he was one of those killed - he said it was OK by him.'

'Do you remember this man's name?'

'Fraid not. Never knew it. He had red hair - that's all I remember about him.'

Chris's head was swimming as he tried to assess the implications of what Freshwater had said. If it was true, he could find no conceivable explanation. The Aussie sat in silence; he seemed to be a man who was able to take his time about things.

'Sorry,' Freshwater said eventually. 'This is a bit painful for you, I guess.'

'It is, yes, but it's more than that...I'm just baffled. What about the bodies? They must have only found six.'

'I suppose so. It's a poser all right.'

'I think most of the dead were horribly burned. Could that be it?'

The tough-man Aussie exterior was softened by an undisguised sense of sympathy. 'I don't think it could,' Freshwater said reluctantly. 'I know this is gruesome for you, son, but...well, they may have been unrecognisable, but you couldn't get the actual number of bodies mixed up.' He looked at Chris with concern. 'I'm sort of sorry I brought this up. I'd no idea there was a mix-up - if there was one. I expect they asked me some questions back then, before I left UK, but...I was in no state. I can't have been very helpful. Then when you get home you want to put these matters out of your mind, till you're ready to face up to them again. Guess I've just about reached that point.'

That all but exhausted the matter, but Freshwater seemed in no hurry to go and the pair sat on for a few minutes in a silence that was almost companionable. A murmur of voices reached them from the churchyard. After a bit the Australian wrote something on a piece of paper and handed it over.

'Here's where I'll be in London for the next two weeks, in case you want to ask me something else. And my address in Australia. Hope you'll come and see me there one day.'

'Thank you. I'm so grateful to you for this information.'

'I bet.' Freshwater laughed. 'You just don't know what to do with it, eh? Look, I'll need to tell the authorities about this, now I know something's amiss. Have to decide what, exactly. I'll give you a ring before I leave UK, and we can talk it over.'

They had already stood up to go when Chris remembered something else. 'Oh - you said something about a dog?'

Freshwater clicked his fingers. 'Yeah, that's right. Nearly forgot. There was a dog on board.'

'On the plane?'

He grinned at his companion's astonishment. 'It happened

- you'd be amazed. Not sure about this, but I think it belonged to your Dad.'

'A dog!' Chris said. 'All these surprises. I can hardly take them in.'

'I don't wonder.'

'But what became of it? There was no mention of a dog in the accident report.'

'There wouldn't be, would there,' Freshwater said, giving a leery look. 'Dogs weren't allowed on RAF aircraft.'

'Oh - I see what you mean. Maybe it just got burnt to a frazzle, poor devil.'

'Possible. Though it's a funny thing - those little mothers do better in crashes than we do, don't know why. If I'd had to put money on something surviving, I'd have put it on the dog.'

A shadow fell across the nave, and David Threlfall appeared in the doorway. 'There you are, you two,' he said. 'The party's beginning to break up out there. Ben Silver is asking after you, Chris. I gather he's invited you back for a cup of tea.'

'He has,' Chris said. 'But first of all there's someone he's just got to meet.' He asked Freshwater to accompany him, and went out to apologise to Ben Silver for keeping him waiting.

The old man was standing on his own by the yew tree. 'Tek yer time,' he said. 'There's no rush. I've nothing else to do.'

'Before we leave,' Chris said, 'There's something important.' He turned to Freshwater. 'Sorry to spring this on you. You had a surprise for me - now I've got one for you. Peter - this is Ben Silver. He's the man who pulled you out of the burning Lancaster twenty years ago.'

Even the laid-back Aussie found this a moment of high emotion. Silver was equally overcome. They shook hands but neither of them was able to get any words out. Freshwater rubbed at his eyes with the back of a hand. Eventually he managed to speak, in a gruff voice.

'Mr Silver - I owe you everything,' he said simply, moving forward to embrace the farmhand's unsteady figure.

The scene was so intense that Chris felt his presence was intrusive, and he left them alone for a moment. Most of the local people had drifted away by now, and there were just a handful of visitors left in the churchyard. The researcher Christian Smythe came up and said his goodbyes, followed by Derry Holmes the stone mason. Alison materialised, and took Chris's arm.

'What a lovely day,' she said. 'Congratulations.'

'I've just heard something really strange,' Chris said. 'Can't wait to tell you about it.'

'At home, though. We have to be going. Dad's getting very fretful.'

He saw Susan cross the churchyard to collect Reg, who was on his own, gazing disconsolately at a gravestone. Alison went over to join them.

'Chris?'

He turned to find his father's old airforce friend standing nearby. The man held out a hand. 'Freddy Mitchell.'

'Mr Mitchell - I'm so sorry. We've been here all afternoon and I've not said a word.'

'Don't worry. You've been busy. And so have I. I've been gossiping with your mother.'

'I know but...oh, this is too bad. I really wanted to talk to you. And now I've got to go off with someone else. One of the local people has asked me for tea. He's already been waiting patiently for me.'

'Look, we need more time than we're going to get here,' Freddy said. The former engineer looked careworn and none too well, but also very friendly; Chris liked him immediately. 'Come and see me, will you?' he went on. 'I'm only in the Midlands. We'll give it a whole afternoon. Ring me. You've got the number.'

'I'd really like to do that,' Chris said. 'I'll do it this week.'

'Super. Make sure you do. I'll be off, then.'

He was half way to his car when Chris called out and stopped him in his tracks. 'Mr Mitchell. Just one thing. Did my father have a dog?'

'A dog! I'll say he did,' Freddy called, across the twenty yards that separated them. 'Bitsa. A lovely hound. I'll tell you all about her.' With that he turned and plodded rather heavily back to his car.

~ Fourteen ~

18 September 1964

Hard as he was pressed, Freshwater could not be persuaded to go back to Ben Silver's, so Chris went on his own. As he had promised, Silver put his daughter into Chris's car, and she gave directions to the house, which was in a village a few miles away. The daughter, a chubby woman in her thirties, was friendly but didn't have much conversation, so Chris was left with his thoughts as they chugged through the Cambridgeshire countryside.

And what thoughts they were. The day had gone well - no doubt about that - but Peter Freshwater's quiet materialisation beside the memorial stone had been a bombshell. Chris's brain was still grappling with the new information Freshwater had provided. A man and a dog short! The Australian seemed so sure about the extra man, yet no explanation that Chris could devise would fit that new version of events. Was it possible that Christian Smythe's researches had overlooked some vital fact, or that the RAF's public archives omitted sensitive material, which was held somewhere in secret files? And if there was a seventh man, what had happened to the body? Surely a man's remains, however badly burnt, could not be concealed or overlooked?

'Here we are.'

Silver's daughter pointed to the driveway of a cottage in an ordinary-looking village street. When Chris had parked she led the way inside, to a lounge where Ben Silver and his wife were waiting. The room was a basic affair, long lived in, with no pretence at even the most basic decorative effect. Despite the warmth of the day, a small wood fire was burning in the grate. Also present were two unkempt dogs of a long-haired variety, and a cat which apparently shared their space in harmony. The cavernous armchairs were coated in animal hairs.

Mr Silver had levered himself out of one of the chairs as

Chris entered. Frail as he was, the labourer had a fierce enough handshake. His rough palm grated against Chris's soft, city-dweller skin.

Silver sat Chris down and sent his daughter into the kitchen to make tea. 'I remember that plane coming down like it were yesterday,' he said, without preamble.

'Did you actually see it happen, Mr Silver?'

'I saw it,' he said. 'I were in the fields, late afternoon. Heard the noise. They make a mighty roar, them big Lancasters. Came over the farm house - only just cleared that, you know - past water tower. Her wing caught the edge of the wood. Round she went, ploughed straight into trees. Terrible noise, she made.' Silver shuddered, though he was the last man to go in for dramatic effects. 'We saw the flames shoot up straight away.'

'They told me you went to help,' Chris said.

'I weren't the only one. There were five or six on us. You saw people running across the fields to the wood. Couple of men from the estate office were nearest.'

Silver's daughter came in with the tea, and he broke off for a moment while that was sorted out. Chris managed to conceal his impatience.

'Could you tell me what happened when you got there?,' he said eventually.

'Trees smashed down everywhere on the edge of Potton,' Silver said. 'Bits of plane all over the ground. No doubt where she was, all right. You could see the flames - hear 'em too. Those two fellers from the office were there, but they were just stood by, lookin' on.' He shook his head at the memory. 'You could see men in the wreckage, an' one of 'em was moving.'

'Dad went straight in,' his daughter said, speaking unexpectedly. 'People were afraid but Dad just went on in and pulled the man out. Mum told me all about it.' They looked across to where her mother sat silent, engulfed in a sofa, hugging herself. 'She used to tell me,' the daughter added. 'She don't talk much now.'

'Mr Taylor, he helped me,' said Silver. 'The man's clothes were burning. Like a torch, 'e was. Cryin' out. Terrible. We pulled him clear. Mr Taylor - he was wearing a jacket - he took it off and rolled the man in it, put out the flames.' Again he broke off, obviously disturbed by the recollection. 'Lyin' on ground, smoulderin'. You can't believe it, Mr Nash, that a man can survive, but he did. They took 'im off to hospital. Didn't see 'im no more...'

'Until today.'

'That's right.' Silver's voice cracked slightly. 'We heard 'e'd got better, but never saw no more till today 'e comes back. Can't rightly believe it. It were a good thing you did, Mr Nash, this memorial. Good fer all o'us.'

There were questions Chris longed to ask, but Silver seemed overwrought - and he was, Chris guessed, a man who rarely gave way to emotion. His daughter came across to sit on the edge of his chair and put an arm round her father's shoulders. 'All right, Dad.'

'What happened then, Mr Silver?' Chris said eventually. 'Could you tell me?'

He saw the same expression he'd noticed up at the church, as if there were things Silver could not bring himself to remember. He hesitated, not wanting to trouble the man or put his health in jeopardy. He gave the daughter a very direct look.

'Maybe I shouldn't ask...' he said. 'If it's going to be upsetting.'

'Oh, dad's all right,' the woman said. 'It's about you. He's worried about you.'

It was a disturbing moment. Chris felt embarrassment that he had misinterpreted the signs while the daughter had understood, but also a sort of fear, knowing that what Silver had to say would be hard to bear. But there was no stopping now. 'I really need to know, Mr Silver,' he urged.

'I suppose you do at that,' Silver said, 'An I ain't no right ter keep it to meself. But it's not a nice story lad, understand that.' He shifted in the armchair and went on heavily. 'There were two men in the pilot seats. One of 'em was dead. I could see that straight away. Head smashed in where it'd hit the instrument panel. One of the Australians - you could see the uniform. The other pilot...'

'Yes.'

'He were injured all right, but still conscious...burning...calling out for help. Oh, it was terrible.' He shook his head from side to side. 'I couldn't get 'im free. I tried, but 'e was trapped somehow, and no-one would help me. They wouldn't come in. Afterwards they said they thought there were bombs on board, but there couldn't'ave bin, course not. I could've freed 'im, if only they'd've helped me.'

There was real anguish in Silver's voice; it was as though he was there at the site of the accident, 20 years after the event.

'Dad got burnt bad,' his daughter put in, clearly anxious to exonerate her father from any blame. 'He was in hospital for weeks after. He tried all he could.'

'Of course he did,' Chris said. Of course. No-one else did what he tried to do.'

'I've never got that poor man out of my head,' said Silver. He was lost in his memories, almost oblivious to Chris's presence; had forgotten his earlier concern for the impact his words might have. 'Never seen a man die before that. Crying out. Burning like a torch. Strange thing was that 'e 'ad red hair, and that was all flaming too.'

Chris looked up sharply, stirred from the scarcely bearable thoughts of his father's agony. 'No, no, Mr Silver - he didn't have red hair.'

'What's that?' Silver raised his head too, jolted from his memories.

'That must be wrong, about the red hair.'

'No lad, it was red all right.'

'My father had dark hair.'

Silver stared, and Chris could see the obstinacy in the man's character. 'It was red,' he said with finality. 'I won't forget that, will I?'

An awkward silence came between them. Silver was obviously put out at being doubted. Chris tried to focus on what the labourer had said. As in the churchyard, with Freshwater, he was finding it hard to absorb information that didn't fit the accident report.

'Could it have been one of the Australians?' he said eventually.

Silver shook his head. 'He was English. Well...he was RAF. He had the uniform.'

Chris put a hand out to touch the man's arm. 'I'm sorry, Mr Silver. I'm sorry to have doubted you. Of course you know what happened, better than anyone. It's just...I don't understand. My father was the pilot of that plane, and he didn't have red hair.'

'Then that weren't your father,' Silver said with complete certainty. 'Any road, your father wasn't in the pilot's seat.'

Chris sat with his heart thumping furiously in his chest and his brain in utter confusion. Whatever Silver's testimony meant, it gave the lie to official versions of the accident. He gave up on the questions and they sat a while in silence. He took a good look at Ben Silver, wishing he had more experience than twenty-one years could give. It wasn't easy making a judgement of character when you're hardly out of school, especially this character, so different in background and experience from his own. Silver had been strong in physique and strong in personality; a difficult man, in all probability - a man who knew his own mind. He was ill now, and in decline, but there was no suggestion of mental infirmity. When he said red hair you believed him.

'Mr Silver, you've been so helpful,' Chris said at last. 'Did you ever tell anyone else about this - I mean the pilot having red hair?'

'Don't reckon I did,' the labourer said. 'No-one ever asked me.'

'No, of course not. You don't happen to remember, do you, how many men were in the plane when it crashed?'

He thought for a moment. 'Don't think I can say that, Mr Nash. Supposed to be six, weren't there?'

'That's what the report said, but I wondered whether you noticed.'

'I don't rightly know,' he said. 'Too much going on. I think there were five bodies taken to the office, as well as Mr Freshwater, who we got out. I can't say for sure.'

Chris stood up, ready to go, but as he did so one of the long-haired dogs sleeping by the fire pricked up its ears at a sound from the garden and let out a low, half-waking growl.

'Shush, Smut,' said Silver's wife, speaking for the first time from the depths of her armchair.

'There is another thing I wanted to ask,' Chris said. 'I know this sounds odd, but did you see a dog on the plane?'

'A dog!'

'Yes. Was there any sign of one?'

'A dog.' There was just the suggestion of a smile on Silver's lips. 'Weren't no dog, Mr Nash. Not on a plane.'

~ Fifteen ~

September 1964

Chris drove back to London that evening with a lot on his mind. At home, he saw that Alison was in her room and went straight in to see her. He repeated all the details of his conversations with Peter Freshwater and Ben Silver.

'It's a poser all right,' Alison said. She jumped up from the bed, where she had been reclining full length, and leaned back with her elbows on the window sill. Unusually, she gave the information quite lengthy consideration before offering any opinion at all. 'One thing we know for sure now,' she said at last, 'There was a red-headed man on board, and a pilot at that. Both the Australian and the farm labourer bloke have separately identified him. Even though he wasn't in the accident records.'

'Yes. Who the hell was he? And if the man *was* on board, how could he have just disappeared like that without getting chased down by the RAF?'

'Do you have any clues about that?' she asked.

Chris shook his head. 'I'll ask Freddy Mitchell. He said I could go and see him. You know - my father's flight engineer. He was there at the memorial service.'

'Oh, I know Freddy.' Alison suffered a minor outbreak of her legendary giggling. 'He spent most of the time up there chattering to Mum. I could swear she was flirting with him. I've never seen her quite like that.' She pulled a wry expression. 'Poor Dad. He felt right out of it.'

'Oh. I suppose you're sorry I started all this,' Chris said.

'No, I'm not,' she said firmly, back to her usual custom of having a well thought-out opinion ready. 'You need to know the full story, and so do they. Let's have it out in the open.' She spoke with unusual passion. 'You know I've realised - ever since you found out what happened back then - how much this has been bugging them. They've let it fester away for 20 years. It's not healthy.'

'I s'pose not. So...do you think I should tell Mum what I've just told you?'

'That's more difficult, isn't it. What we know, it's so confusing. Perhaps leave it until you're a bit clearer - if you ever are.'

'Don't remind me. It's like a riddle.'

Alison paced around the room for a bit in her flat-footed way. Her pale face looked thoughtful. Chris was beginning to realise how much he leaned on her for moral support, especially since he'd parted company with Melanie.

'Chris, I was wondering...' she said.

'What?'

'I know this is difficult for you. I was wondering if you thought...well, because the red-headed pilot was on the plane, that perhaps your father wasn't. I wondered...maybe you've even been hoping your father could still be alive?'

'I know,' Chris said. The thought was out in the open now, and he was glad of it. 'I hardly dared to think that, but of course it has been in the back of my mind. It'd be silly, wouldn't it?'

'No, it wouldn't, she said, putting both arms round his waist and resting her head on his shoulder. 'It'd be only natural. As long as you know that it's not very likely.'

'Don't worry,' he said. It's not possible - I know that. Sadly. I'm being realistic about this, even if I do have my dreams.'

Next day Chris telephoned Freddy Mitchell, who said he could visit at any time. They fixed it for two days later. Mitchell invited him to stay the night, but Chris thought he could get up to the Midlands and back again in a day, if Clara were up to it.

On that day Clara behaved impeccably, even on the M1

motorway, which Chris was experiencing for the first time – and where the Austin 10's sedate bodywork and limited horsepower seemed out of place. Freddy Mitchell lived in a village near Loughborough. The approach was by a bridge across the river Soar, where a row of fishermen were lined up on the bank casting lines into the water. Mitchell's house was in the oldest road in the village, near to the parish church. Chris parked Clara in the narrow street and was met by Freddy at the front door. There was something reassuring about the man's bulk and his welcoming smile, though Chris also detected, even on such short acquaintance, an underlying air of sadness. Mitchell's wife Sheila was a red-headed Irish woman who had clearly been very attractive in her recent past. She looked as if she was putting on too much weight and gave an immediate impression of being highly strung.

She left the two of them to drink tea in the lounge.

'You know I was a close friend of your father's,' Freddy said, as soon as they were alone together.

'Mum told me. I'd love to know more and...what he was really like. When was the last time you saw him?'

'That would be soon after our last flight together - September 1944, late one evening. He kissed me as we lay on the ground outside my quarters. Or so I was told afterwards,' Freddy added hastily, seeing Chris's look of mild consternation. 'We were both the worse for wear at the time.'

He went on to describe his first meeting with Gregson and the many operational trips they'd made together, and recounted what he could remember (which wasn't a lot) about the last mess party.

'Then off he went to Bassingbourn,' Freddy said. 'And I didn't see John again.'

'Were you surprised when you heard about the accident?'

'Deeply shocked but not surprised, Chris. You know, about one in ten of the airmen who lost their lives during the war were killed in training accidents? It was all too common.'

Chris couldn't help himself, and plunged straight in with the questions that were burning his tongue. He described what Freshwater had said at the church ceremony - and Ben Silver after him - about a red-haired pilot being on the last flight.

Freddy's reaction was instantaneous. He jerked upright in his seat and muttered a single word: '*Stephens*!'

Chris looked at him. 'What? Stephens? Who's that?'

'Patrick Stephens. Oh, my goodness, Chris.'

'Stephens? You knew this man?'

Chris could see Freddy trying to rein himself in, assuming a cautious look. 'Let's be careful here. Perhaps I shouldn't jump to conclusions, but it's hard not to.' He thought for a moment, then decided to offload what was on his mind. 'Take this with a big pinch of salt, Chris, but I have to say it. There was an Irish pilot at Mepal called Patrick Stephens. Very popular chap and a good pilot - if a bit wild at times. The thing is - *he* had red hair. He transferred to Bassingbourn at almost the same time as your father. Dear oh dear.'

'But...wouldn't people have noticed...if he disappeared.'

'He did disappear,' Freddy said grimly. 'That's the point. I heard something about it, though I was no longer at the same base. The RAF thought he'd gone AWOL. Are you familiar with that expression - absent without leave?'

'I know.'

'It happened quite a lot in the war, to all sorts of people - and Stephens was the unpredictable type.'

'But...isn't it odd that this didn't come out at the time – in the accident report?'

Freddy gave it some thought. 'It is a bit,' he said. 'The oddest thing is that Stephens wasn't listed amongst the crew members - that is, assuming he *was* on board. Someone should have remembered from the ground crew.' He pondered again. 'But this bit of intelligence has emerged - that is, if there's anything in it - because you've made some enquiries from the ground level up. The RAF obviously didn't interview this farm labourer chap - and Freshwater would have been too shaken up to give them reliable information. All the same...'

'Do you know if Stephens was married?' Chris said.

Freddy shot him a glance from over his glasses. 'I know what you're thinking. I'm pretty sure he wasn't. But there'd be someone who needs to know, even now...mother or father, a brother maybe.'

'What do you think I should do?'

He thought again. 'It's a poser, isn't it. You could just turn the whole thing over to the RAF people.'

'I don't want to do that,' Chris said, very quickly. 'Not yet.' At that moment he couldn't have explained why he said so; it was something felt rather than thought.

Freddy gave his companion a long, hard look. 'Then I think the first thing is to try and establish whether Stephens ever turned up again. You'd look pretty silly if you came up with this theory, then found Stephens had been living the life of Riley all this time back in Ireland.

'I can see that. But I've no idea where to find him.'

'Will you leave that to me? All RAF fliers had to leave a 'next of kin' address - still do. I can find that out without starting any hares running. Still know someone in Personnel. Mind you, after twenty years the address may not be much use to you.'

They broke off for a moment as Freddy's wife came in with a query about lunch: did they want to eat in the house?...she had to nip out and might be delayed...there wasn't a great deal in the fridge...and so on. It sounded like a lot of fuss about nothing, and she managed to appear ponderous and edgy at one and the same time. Freddy was patient with her; checked with Chris, then said they'd have a sandwich at a local pub.

'Let's take the dog for a walk while we're about it,' he said.

Freddy had a curious-looking dog, a mongrel of very mixed provenance. They led it onto a path alongside the canal, past a little marina full of moored barges and then to a bridge over a large weir. Freddy leant over a wooden fence to watch the weir, as the turbulent water rushed away beneath them. The dog stood patiently beside him.

'You're not married, Chris?'

'No.'

'Thinking of it?'

'I was, sort of - but that fell apart.'

He grunted. 'What's your theory about your Dad and Stephens, and all that? Do you have one?'

'I couldn't help wondering,' Chris said, 'If my father ever got on that plane at all.'

'Thought so. I don't blame you. It just wasn't your Dad's style though, to miss a flight in that way. He'd have been on it, you know - I feel pretty sure about that.'

He saw Chris's face fall. 'Chris, I don't know what happened any more than you do. There's something strange about this, that's for sure, but you mustn't start thinking your Dad is alive. He isn't.'

'I know, I know. Alison - my sister - she's already been on to me about that.'

'And if he is, I'll want to know why the bugger hasn't got in touch with me all these years. There's another thing,' Freddy said, picking up a small stick and hurling it into the water below the weir. 'If your Dad *were* alive - just supposing - he wouldn't be the man that everyone remembers.' His features assumed a faraway, brooding appearance. 'All those young tearaways, the life and death heroics, the waggling wings, the uniforms - God, how they loved the uniforms. When the war ended, most of us had a hell of a time adjusting.'

'Age shall not weary them,' Chris said, recalling the closing words of the memorial service.

Freddy smiled sadly. 'Nor the years condemn.' He straightened up, and rested both hands on his stomach, which bulged out over the top of his trousers. The dog looked quizzically up at him. 'You wouldn't believe it now - I was quite a lad during the war. Used to sport a damn great handlebar moustache. I was a bit older than your father and most of the boys. They thought I knew what life was all about. Did I hell?' He laughed, though it sounded like a cry of mortification. 'We were all potty about flying. It was madness. Everybody loved us. There's something very loveable about a young man who's about to die. I met Sheila during the war, towards the end of it. She'd have walked through fire for me then.'

Chris said 'What did you do after the war, Mr Mitchell.'

'Pilots they didn't want,' he said, and bitterness surged out again. 'I got a job in a factory, assembling aeroplanes. Had to be near 'em, you see. No glamour there. Money was indifferent. Sheila got unhappy. Then we upped sticks and came out here. I run a little shop in the village mending televisions and Hoovers. Found my level at last.'

He gave the dog a tug on its lead and they started back along the path, away from the weir. 'Your father's dog,' he said. 'Why did you ask me about that, back at the service?'

'I was going to ask you again. The Australian - Freshwater - he said there was a dog on the plane.'

Freddy stopped in his tracks and looked at his companion another direct look. 'That's something else then,' he said slowly. 'Your father did have a dog. It was called Bitsa.'

'Bitsa? What kind of name is that?'

'B-I-T-S-A.' Freddy spelt it out. 'It meant 'bits of this and bits of that - half Labrador and half something else. I was almost as fond of the dog as he was. Not like this silly thing.' He pretended to give his mongrel a kick. 'When I heard John had been killed I went across to Bassingbourn to find it. No trace. His orderly wasn't on duty, but there was a story going round that the dog had gone up in the Lanc. I'm sure that wasn't mentioned in the accident report.'

'No.'

'No, of course not.' His face held an expression of pure cynicism. 'Hmm. She was a super dog, Bitsa.'

They'd reached a small pub by the riverside, with tables and seats outside it next to the river bank. Freddy tied the dog up to one of the tables and went inside, insisting on paying for the sandwiches and the beer. He came out carrying a saucer and poured some beer into it for the dog.

'Did Bitsa drink beer?' Chris said.

'How did you guess?'

They sat for a while in companionable silence. Freddy gazed into the depths of the river, clearly a long way away in his thoughts. The sadness came off him like something that could be touched.

'What are you going to do about all this?' Freddy said eventually , leaning across the wooden table. 'I'll look up an address for Stephens. But do you have other ideas?'

'Not really,' Chris admitted. 'I'm stuck. What else can I do?'

'There is one other possibility.' Freddy pursed his lips, as if there was something he didn't want to rake up. 'Look, I'm not saying there's anything to know about John's death except what we already know. But still...if there's anyone alive now who knows more...well, there *was* a woman he met. I just have a feeling about her.'

'Sarah,' Chris said.

Freddy stared at him, astonished. 'You know about that!'

'My mother told me. She found out about her the day before my father died.'

'The silly bugger,' he exclaimed. 'Wouldn't you know it. I could see he was headed for trouble. I tried to warn him off, you know.' In spite of the stern words, he smiled at the memory. 'God, she was attractive, though. More than flesh and blood could bear.'

'Is there any chance I could track her down, do you think?'

'I doubt it,' he said. 'And she probably doesn't know anything anyway. But it's all you've got.'

'Do you remember her second name?'

'Sarah Frielen. F-R-I-E-L-E-N. Of course she may be a married woman by now. But she was an actress then, so she could have kept her maiden name. There's something else I remember. We met her in Cambridge, but her parents' home was in the Lake District. Grasmere, to be exact.'

'That's really helpful,' Chris said. 'What a memory you've got. After all, this happened more than twenty years ago.'

'There's a reason for it. I really fancied her myself.' He looked around cautiously as he said it, as if his wife might be hiding behind one of the nearby bushes. 'John and I visited her dressing room at the theatre. He was the one she took a shine to. She wrote to him, invited him out. Poor chap, he was like a lamb to the slaughter. Tell you the truth, I was quite put out. I thought she'd taken to me. She was an absolute cracker.' For a moment he resembled a much younger man. He raised his glass. 'To you, Chris. And to the success of your investigations.'

~ Sixteen ~

October 1964

After seeing Freddy Mitchell, Chris was tied up for several days with visits to his college, as he prepared to start there in October. He'd been fortunate that, thus far, investigating his father's death had coincided with some free months before the course. But now he could feel time running out. There were a mere couple of weeks left before he'd find himself fully occupied on other matters.

Talking to Freddy had left him with two possible (albeit remote) leads to follow: the Irish pilot, Pat Stephens, and the actress Sarah Frielen. He didn't have an address between them. He felt that the matter of Stephens's possible involvement should be cleared up first, though it promised to shed no further light on his father. So he was pleased that towards the end of the week there was a phone call from Freddy giving a 'next of kin' contact for Pat Stephens. It was an address in Frederick Street, Belfast.

Freddy had reminded him that the information dated from 1944, and Chris thought it unlikely that members of the Stephens family would be still living there. But when he phoned Directory Enquiries a voice immediately confirmed that a Stephens was in residence, and gave the telephone number.

He stared at that number for some time, weighing the options in his head, steeling himself to pick up the phone. Belfast was a long way away. If he managed to speak to a Stephens relative he could establish soon enough whether the pilot had ever returned to Belfast. But assuming he hadn't, what then? It would be callous to convey sensitive information about the man's probable death over the telephone lines; after all, Chris was well placed to know how close relatives might react in those circumstances. On the other hand his own amateurish investigation was the last vehicle that family members would appreciate as the basis for such desperate information. One way or another he risked giving offence. It was enough to make him think of passing the whole business over to the RAF, to let them to sort it out.

But Chris didn't do that. He lifted the receiver and dialled the number. A woman's voice answered immediately.

He gave his name. 'I'm trying to contact someone who

knew an RAF pilot called Patrick Stephens,' he said.

There was an unnerving silence, and when the woman answered, her voice sounded different. 'We haven't seen Pat in a long time,' she said. Her Irish accent was so strong he could hardly make the words out.

'No.' He hesitated, unsure how to go on. 'Can I ask - are you related to him?'

'I'm his sister.'

'Look - could I come and see you about this?' he said.

'Who are you?' Now her tone had hardened and was full of mistrust. 'Are you from the RAF?'

'Nothing like that. I'm sorry - this is such a difficult call to make. My father was killed in a plane crash in 1944, at the end of the war. I've only just been told. I've been trying to discover more about it and I...a couple of people mentioned your brother's name. I wanted to tell you what they said. Could I come?'

'I see.' Her voice had softened again; it was her barometer of emotional response. 'I'm sorry to hear about your father. When did he have his accident exactly, could you tell me?'

'It was September. September 1944.'

This time her silence was even longer, and suddenly Chris was sure that she knew Stephens was dead. He felt an inglorious surge of relief because his task had been made easier. He wasn't used to being the bearer of bad news.

'You said your name was Chris?' she said at length.

'Yes.'

'I'm Mary. Where do you live?'

'I'm in London.'

'It's an awful long way to come, Chris, to tell me something I know already, in my bones.'

'I'd like to come - if it's all right.'

'Of course it's all right. I need to hear it. I've waited a long time.'

They agreed he would call the day after next, which gave him time to arrange the trip. Chris had never been to Ireland before, but the journey looked straightforward enough. He told his mother he'd be away for a couple of days and took the train to Liverpool, then went across on the night ferry. In the darkness he stood at the front of the boat watching spray spring up from the surface of the sea. Then he went down into the big communal cabin, where the atmosphere was stuffy and the engine sound reverberated in the enclosed space. A few people were scattered about on the wooden seating, most of them asleep; Chris eventually followed suit, using his overnight bag as a pillow.

It was just after eight when the ferry docked at Belfast. Drizzle fell from a grey sky and the streets looked raw and unlovely. Chris went into a rough-looking cafe and downed several cups of coffee and some rounds of toast. After that he called in to a newsagent's shop and bought a map of Belfast. The plan had been to take a cab to Mary Stephens's address, but Frederick Street was so near the harbour that walking was the obvious way of getting there. He passed under the harbour rail link and walked through the dowdy streets, feeling a growing apprehension about the task ahead.

The house had a front door that had not seen a coat of paint in twenty years. Mary Stephens answered his knock. Chris thought she was probably in her late thirties, a thin, poorly dressed woman with sloping shoulders. Her face looked pale and washed out, but she had a head of flame-red hair.

'Mary?'

'Yes.'

'I'm Chris Nash.'

'Good Lord, Chris, you look as if you've slept on a park bench,' she said.

'I have, more or less.'

The house had a drab, abandoned air. The whole place was enfolded in a deep silence. As they went down the hall, past the living room, Chris saw an old woman sitting motionless in an armchair, staring at the wall. Mary took his arm and led him on into a small kitchen. She motioned him to sit at one side of a wooden table, and she sat facing.

He was grateful to her; she made it easy for him. 'Now tell me please, Chris,' she said in her fierce Irish brogue. 'Tell me how Pat died.'

He told his story: how he learnt of his father's death, the

memorial ceremony at Cockayne Hatley, the conversations with Peter Freshwater and Ben Silver, then Freddy Mitchell. The one thing he left out was Silver's description of her brother burning and crying for help; he knew better than anyone that she would not want to hear that. As he spoke she gripped his hand on the table. She said nothing but her bloodless lips twisted, and tears rolled down her face to fall onto the wooden table top.

'I can't say for sure it was your brother,' he concluded. 'But I'm afraid it seems the most likely explanation. I thought you'd want to know. I'm so sorry.'

'I think I've always known.' She wiped her face with her hands, leaving a dark streak across one cheek. 'We had the authorities round here after Pat disappeared - and more than once since. I wondered if it was them again when you rang. They thought he'd done a runner. There were pilots who did that, I know. Not him. My mother never stopped believing Pat was alive. Now, poor thing, she wouldn't recognise Pat if he walked through that door. I didn't tell her, but I knew he was dead. He'd never have let us suffer all these years.'

Chris went across to the sink and filled the kettle from the cold water tap. The tinkling sound seemed unnaturally loud, breaking the silence . His gesture seemed quite natural, though he'd been in her house but twenty minutes. They had a shared sense of loss. 'Can I make you a cup of tea?' he said.

'A cup of tea is it, Chris?' Without warning Mary's face screwed up again and her shoulders heaved silently. While she recovered he lit the gas and found the teapot and some cups. 'Silly,' she said eventually. 'I'm not used to people doing things for me. My mother's so helpless now.'

He took the tea over and faced her again across the table.

'How old were you when your brother disappeared?'

'I was nineteen. He was my big brother. I adored him.'

'I'm sorry.'

'It's all right. I just needed to cry.'

'Yes.'

They had some tea together, and then some more. He'd have liked to stay longer, and thought she would have welcomed it too, but found himself at the front door. They had nothing in common but the bond of their shared loss.

'I don't know what to do about all this,' Chris said, on the doorstep. 'I'm still not clear about what happened. Not exactly. I suppose eventually I'll have to inform the RAF people.'

'You do what you think, Chris,' she said. 'It'll make no difference to me.'

'But, if they think he...he ran away...' He couldn't bring himself to use the word 'deserted'. 'It would clear that up, at least.'

'I don't care what anyone thinks. There's only me. And I know.' She took his arm. 'Thank you for coming here to tell me. I wouldn't have wanted to hear it from some official.'

He thought for a moment. 'Mary...I wonder if you'd like to visit Potton Wood some day? See where it happened? It's a nice place. I could meet you at Liverpool and drive you there.'

She stood looking down at the door-step, and he thought she was going to say 'no'. But she spoke out more strongly than before. 'I think I would like to do that. I'd have to get Mum looked after, but that would be possible. Yes, I'd like to very much.'

~ Seventeen ~

October 1964

Up to that point Chris had explored the circumstances of his father's death in a logical way, taking each new clue as it surfaced and making a measured response to it. Now, for the first time, he acted on impulse. He had taken his leave of Mary Stephens before lunch and boarded the return ferry to Liverpool. In the evening, at Liverpool's Lime Street station, he was scanning the return train times to London when he saw the place name 'Kendal' up on the board. 'Kendal, gateway to the Lake District,' the posters often said. Into his brain rushed Freddy's words about Sarah Frielen. 'Her parents' home was in the Lake District...Grasmere, to be exact.' It dawned upon him that Liverpool wasn't very far from the Lake District - certainly a giant stride towards it if you were starting from London.

He went to the information desk and found that the nearest you could get to Grasmere by rail was Windermere, just North of Kendal, after which local buses would take over. He was almost on automatic pilot now, and without further thought bought the ticket and took the first available train North. When he jumped out onto the platform at Windermere Station, after one change of train, it was dark. The previous night's half-sleep on the ferry was taking its toll and Chris felt he couldn't stay awake a moment longer. He walked down the road outside the station, took the first cheap bed-and-breakfast place that presented itself, and got his head down.

He woke late the next morning, only just in time for the tail-end of breakfast, as the rather unfriendly landlady made clear. Eating a piece of cold toast under her censorious eye, he began to feel that the previous night's impulse was a foolish wild goose chase. He had little enough to show for his wanderings around the British Isles, and the Lake District was the craziest stab of all. He knew no-one there, and could almost as easily have carried out enquiries about Sarah Frielen from London. But to have gone home at this point would have made him feel still more foolish, so he went out and caught a bus bound for Ambleside, and then another to Grasmere.

He reached the town in less than an hour. Though the main tourist season was over there were still people around, browsing in gift shops or taking a mid-morning drink in Grasmere's cafes. But it was the surrounding landscape that caused Chris to stop and stare: the freshness in the air, clarity of definition, the sheer greenness, so foreign to a long-time resident of North London. Had he not been in Grasmere on a mission he would have relished rambling through the countryside; perhaps even scaling one of the peaks visible in the distance.

Instead he asked for directions to the post office, and went in there to consult a telephone directory. The absurdity of his impulsive dash North weighed heavily as he leafed through the bulky volume. He had a single clue: this Sarah woman's surname of Frielen. Drawing a blank with the name would leave him without further options. He would be back on the train to London and none the wiser.

It was with some relief therefore that Chris found the area was not entirely devoid of Frielens. Half a dozen of them were listed in the county as a whole, though of these only a single name appeared against a Grasmere address. He copied down the details of all six and asked the postmistress for directions to the local one.

It turned out to be a cottage not far from the centre of the town. In no time Chris was standing outside, taking a deep breath and lifting the heavy door knocker. Was this to be the end of the trail, or the start of more surprising revelations? Was he about to set eyes on the celebrated Sarah? ('God, she was attractive,' Freddy had said.) But when the door opened it was a much more mature woman - 60 years old at least - who stood on the threshold. Despite her age she exuded an air of briskness and self-confidence.

'Yes?'

Chris had had much recent experience in putting delicate questions to strangers, but still wasn't sure how to proceed. In the end he told the woman quite simply that he was looking for a Sarah Frielen, and that she used to be an actress.

'That was my daughter,' she replied without hesitation.

'Was?' He felt a lurch of disappointment. 'Isn't she alive?'

The woman smiled. 'No, I meant that isn't her name any more. She's very much alive. But she doesn't live here. Who are you, if I may ask?'

He explained that his father had been a friend of Sarah's years before. 'I'm very anxious to get in touch with her,' he said.

The woman seemed to have some trouble focusing, but still subjected him to a searching look. 'You know, even without my glasses your face seems familiar,' she said.

'Oh.'

She thought for a moment. 'It's unusual, you must admit, your turning up on the doorstep like this, but you don't look like some maniac who's going to get in Sarah's hair.' Chris was again struck by the mother's unusually assured manner; she was, he imagined, someone who was rarely out of countenance. 'Sarah's in Ambleside,' she went on. 'She's lived there for many years now. Do you want the address?'

'Would you mind?'

'I'll jot it down for you. You're more likely to find her during the day than the evening. If you'll give me your name I'll ring and warn her that you're on your way. You are on your way, are you?'

'Yes, I'll go straight there now. My name's Christopher Nash. And thank you. Thank you very much.'

Back he went, on the same bus that had brought him to Grasmere that morning. Once in Ambleside he asked passers-by for directions to the new-found address. He walked there slowly, almost reluctant to arrive. This Sarah - a mere hunch of Freddy Mitchell's, after all - was his last throw of the dice. If he drew a blank here he'd have to come to the end of the trail. If that happened he must come to terms with his father's death and learn to get on with his own life.

She lived on a new estate of semi-detached buildings right at the edge of Ambleside. The area had been thoughtfully designed; each house was fronted by a decent-sized lawn which gave the whole street a green and spacious appearance. He identified the number and was about to ring the bell when something caught his eye in the corner of the lawn. Tucked away almost flush to the front wall of the house was a small wooden plaque with a single word carved on its face: 'Bitsa'.

As he looked at this, gazing without comprehension, Chris heard the front door open behind him. Before he had a chance to turn a woman's voice said 'Christopher Nash, I assume. I've been racking my brains, but I don't remember your father.'

'That's because his name wasn't Nash,' he said, turning to face her.

The woman's voice had the quality of her mother's: the same self-confidence, and in her case a distinctly provocative edge to it. But the moment she saw Chris's face this changed. 'Oh my God,' she said, in a low voice.

'Are you...?' he began, before realising that the mother had not told him Sarah's married name. 'I'm sorry,' he said, 'I don't know your name. *Were* you...Sarah Frielen?'

She was staring as though she had seen a ghost. 'I was. I'm Sarah Gregson.'

Chris couldn't remember exactly what happened next. His first conscious memory was of himself sitting on the front doorstep, head in hands, with the woman beside him.

'You're as white as a sheet,' she was saying. 'Don't go away.' She went back into the house and returned with a glass of water. As he sipped, she put her hands to either side of his head and turned his face towards her - an oddly physical gesture for a complete stranger. She'd taken charge of the situation all right but was also, he felt, just as agitated as he was, in her own way. Confusion was all around. 'My God, you're so like him,' she said. 'Who the hell are you?'

'I'm his son.'

He could see her trying to work it out, and failing. He knew how she felt.

'Are you OK now?' she said.

'I'm all right. Sorry about that.'

'Let's go inside then.'

Her living room was in a state of mild chaos, with theatrical costumes piled on the sofa and a basket of stage props on the hearth. A tailor's dummy stood in the corner. She guided him in, one arm firmly at his elbow, and pointed to a deep armchair.

'Sit there.'

Her tone brooked no refusal. She was clearly used to being in charge. He needed this firmness, because his own brain had virtually seized up.

He sat back and watched as she paced up and down her own living room. This was the woman who had caused all the trouble twenty years earlier. She was about his mother's age and, like his mother, dark-haired and still very slim. There the resemblance ended. Susan had a tentative side to her character, something that was part of her charm. This woman was decisive, almost bossy, in everything she did and said. She knew her own mind and would impose that will on others if she could get away with it. All the same the attraction was obvious, even to someone like Chris who was half her age. She moved about with such freedom, almost prancing around the room. He could imagine her, years earlier, rejecting the mind-set of the war years, embracing the sort of liberated philosophy that was supposedly the prerogative of his own generation. Her face had an animal appeal, undiminished by the rough, pitted skin.

'Tell me about my father,' Chris broke out. 'Is he alive?'

'How do I know?' She stood with her back to the mantelpiece, hands on hips. 'Now you answer my questions. I want to know who you are.'

'I told you - I'm his son.'

'How can you be? How old are you?'

'Twenty-one.'

'Twenty-one. Good grief.' She was looking at him strangely. 'This isn't fair, sending you up here.'

'No-one sent me.'

'I don't care. Who's your mother?'

'Her name's Susan. She was my father's -'

'Susan! It would be her.' She snapped her head to one side with an odd gesture of exasperation, even despair, so much in contrast to her habitual manner. 'Bloody hell! All these years.' She turned on him fiercely. 'Why now? Why didn't you come before?'

'I've only just found out he was my father. They didn't tell me.'

'Who's they?'

'My mother and...her husband.'

'I see.'

'I can tell you about it, if...'

'If I'll just calm down.' She grinned in her wolfish way and again her felt the power of her attraction. 'All right. I suppose it's not your fault. Go on, then. I'll sit down, if that helps.'

He told the whole story then, from start to finish, and to her credit she sat quietly throughout, making only the occasional interjection or clarification. All the time he was talking he wanted her to be the one doing the talking, him to be asking the questions. As soon as he'd finished he said 'Now, I've given you my side. Tell me, please. You said you were Sarah Gregson. What does that mean? Is he...is he alive?'

'I don't know,' she said again.

'What do you mean?'

'I mean I've not had any contact for...oh, ten years at least. Probably he's alive somewhere. Maybe he's dead - it wouldn't surprise me. He felt like dying. I don't know.'

Chris gasped, feeling an astonishing sensation in his chest, like something bursting. He hardly dared to question her further in case he'd misunderstood. She sat looking at him. It seemed like forever.

'So he was alive after the war,' he said at length.

'Yes, he was.' He never forgot the sight and sound of her wolfish lips framing the three simple words.

With her animal instincts she could tell that he needed to be left alone then, and without a word she left the room. He was scarcely aware of it. He was thinking: he's alive, alive, *he's alive*. After a while she came back with two mugs of coffee, and handed Chris one of them.

'He knew nothing about you,' she said. 'I'm sure of that.'

He felt impossibly ambivalent about Sarah, and would remain so, but was always grateful to her for that remark. 'I want to know about the accident,' he burst out. 'Was he on the plane?'

She shook her head. 'You'll have to ask him that, if you can find him. I always promised I'd say nothing about it.' She turned away to look out of the window, and if it hadn't seemed so unlikely, from a hard nut like her, he'd have said that her eyes filled up. 'The last unbroken promise,' she said.

There were so many things he wanted to ask. 'Your name...Gregson?'

'We were married,' she said lightly, as if it was a matter of no consequence. 'Seven years.'

He gazed at her, tongue-tied.

'We both tried hard, I'll say that,' she went on. 'It wasn't easy after the war. But what do you know?' She said it as you would to a child.

'Not much,' Chris said. 'I've learnt a lot, though, in the past three months.'

She gave him an appraising stare. 'I suppose you have at that. Forgive me for saying so, but your mother was a curse upon us. He felt guilty about leaving her and then he wished he hadn't. The longer we stayed together the more I knew it. And as he also felt guilty about being a deserter, he was a bit of a mess.'

'A deserter?' The word sounded ugly in a suburban drawing room.

'Of course. What did you think?'

'I can't think of it like that. He did so much. All those flights over Germany. He'd done enough.'

'That's what I used to tell him. Didn't do any good. He brooded over it more and more. Of course, quite a few servicemen ducked out - but not too many pilots. Pilots were supposed to be special.'

There was something else Chris wanted to know. 'Could I ask...are you still married to him?'

She shook her head. 'Divorced ten years, at least. I just kept the name. Too lazy to change it.' That didn't sound like her at all. 'I've seen other men, if you want to know,' she said. 'Nothing serious. Never fancied another bout of matrimony, thanks all the same.'

'Are you still an actress?'

'Oh no. I was never much good.' Her honesty was quite unsettling. 'When I was your age I had a sort of presence on stage. And I was attractive. Used to get me parts. I knew it wouldn't last. I do the costumes for a local company here. That's why I live in Ambleside - they've always had a repertory company.' She spoke lightly again, but he could see it meant something to her. 'Gets into your bloodstream, the theatre,' she said. 'Like flying.'

'And what did my father do?'

'Ask him,' she said. 'If you can find him. You've got too many questions.'

'I've one more,' Chris persisted. He knew she was about to dismiss him, but felt he was beginning to get the measure of her. 'Bitsa, the dog - was he a black Labrador.'

'Of course.' She grinned. 'Half Labrador. So you know about him?'

'Someone told me.'

Sarah didn't follow this up; she seemed to lack her sex's curiosity about other people. 'A special dog, in more ways than one. I think your father like him more than he liked me. It was strange, but when Bitsa died the marriage seemed to go from bad to worse.' She looked at her watch. 'I need to be at the theatre in half an hour. You've got to go.'

He stood up. 'Just one thing. Do you have an address - for my father?'

She snorted. 'Not so you'd notice.' She went across to a notepad, and copied something down from an address book. 'This was the one I had. Last time I used it was to send the divorce papers. We've not exactly been exchanging Christmas cards. I've no idea where he is now.'

He thanked her and went out into the front garden. Sarah followed almost as an afterthought. She took hold of Chris's arm, pulled him round to face her, and turned her intense gaze upon him. 'We'll not see each other again,' she said. 'If you do catch up with your father, remember this. It wasn't my fault.' Her tone was defiant. 'I loved him as much as a woman can love a man. I just didn't get it back.'

~ Eighteen ~

October 1964

Chris left Sarah's house like a zombie. He went out onto the pavement and stood blinking at the sedate housing estate around him. From Sarah's garden the small head-stone to Bitsa the dog was visible in its setting of border flowers. The conventional surroundings, mundane to the point of innocence, were a cloak for those personal dramas that had stretched back over the past twenty years. Now he knew. The hopes lurking at the back of his mind ever since he'd talked to Peter Freshwater and Ben Silver - hopes damped down by Freddy and Alison, not to mention himself - were turning to reality. His father had lived through the war; in all probability was still alive.

Chris turned away, retracing the route that had led him to Sarah's house. His feet seemed to move of their own volition, independent of thought processes that were, to say the least, in turmoil. The only sensible course of action after the extraordinary meeting with Sarah was to go home and collect his thoughts, then set out systematically to track his father down. But common sense had nothing to do with it. The single thought in his mind was to get straight to the address that Sarah scribbled on a notepad. It was a street in Islington, London. London! His home town, all that time. He might inadvertently have passed his father in the street, sat next to him in a cinema, all without a second glance. He looked at the address again. No telephone number was given, and if there'd been one he wouldn't have used it. He had in his head a foolish, romantic notion: ringing a bell, seeing a door open, his father coming out onto the doorstep, gazing at the son he'd never known.

He reached the station, took a train to Kendal, then the first train South. Even so it was late evening by the time Chris reached the suburb of Islington, and the light was beginning to fail. His destination turned out to be a long, narrow street off the Essex Road. Its cramped appearance was exaggerated by the presence, on either side of the road, of cars densely parked, and unbroken rows of terraced housing. The mud-coloured brick façades rose to four storeys.

The address he'd been given was a basement flat in number 53, one of those residences where half- windows afforded the only light into the dwelling. Chris had never understood how people could bury themselves in the gloom and damp of places like this. Was his father here, immolated for a decade or more in the half-life of an Islington basement? He descended a short flight of steps into the well of the building and rang the door bell, but could see already that the flat was in darkness. Several further rings brought no response. He peered through the inadequate windows seeking some clue to the flat's contents, and thence to the character of its occupant, but the dark interior gave nothing away.

Chris returned to street level and stood on the pavement

wondering what to do. He was loath to leave, yet there seemed no point in hanging about indefinitely. The residents could be on holiday, or returning home very late; for that matter, the flat might be unoccupied. Still he could not tear himself away. There was a Neighbourhood Watch notice pinned to one of the stunted trees on the pavement and, afraid that he might resemble a loitering, would-be house-breaker, he took to walking up and down the street, never letting the basement flat out of his sight. He was on the farthest edge of one of these perambulations when a car came down the road and pulled up near the house. Chris got only the briefest glimpse of the driver before the man disappeared down the steps to the basement of 53. Lights came on in a front window.

Even then Chris delayed before following the new arrival down the basement steps. After the headlong rush from the Lake District he now felt a strange reticence about proceeding; a fear of not finding his father, or worse, of finding and being disappointed. When he'd finally steeled himself to continue he went down the steps like a robot.

As he rang the door bell the thought that predominated was about recognition. Would he know the man who was about to stand before him? Would it be his father? Or a complete stranger, a dead end to his pursuit of past history? And if it was his father, would he recognise the man? He'd seen just a handful of photographs, and they dated back twenty years. But of course he'd forgotten the resemblance between father and son. The light was poor down in the basement well, but the moment the door opened to reveal a dark figure on the step, Chris knew him. By an odd chance the man stood in much the same posture as he had in that very first photograph, given to Chris by his mother. His haggard features were curiously back-lit by the electric light from the hallway. He looked the same and changed; older, and very like his son.

Chris had the advantage. Gregson had opened his door to a late-evening interloper, and his mind was elsewhere.

'Do I know you?' he said, peering more closely.

'In a way you do.' All Chris's long pent-up excitement had ebbed away. Now that the moment had come he felt his turning up unannounced was an immense imposition on the man . 'I'm sorry...just calling like this.'

'That's all right.' Chris was still a stranger, being considerately treated. He *was* a stranger, after all. 'What can I do for you?' the man said.

'There's something I have to tell you - it's something so important to both of us. Could I possibly come in? I know it's late.'

There were many men who would have refused such a request, but Gregson was obviously not one of them. He seemed almost indifferent to the possibility of trouble or danger; someone who went through the motions of life without much caring how it turned out one way or another. He shot a cautious look in Chris's direction but stood back, allowing him to enter, and pointed through a hallway into his front room. They went through together. The place looked uncared for; badly lit and barely furnished. There was little sign of the normal clutter of everyday living. A couple of dishes sat on a small table, with the remains of a meal on them; breakfast, presumably. Chris stood by the window, aware of the man's close scrutiny upon him.

'I'm afraid this may be a shock,' Chris said, breaking into his story without preamble, while they stood there, together but unconnected, like two men in a railway waiting room. 'I think you knew my mother during the war.' His companion stood unmoved, consumed by a vast indifference. 'My mother,' Chris continued. 'Susan Dilly?'

'Susan!' Gregson jumped at the mention of her name.

Now that he'd started, Chris wanted to finish it quickly. He knew himself what it was like taking in a bombshell of this kind. 'You did know her, didn't you?'

The man looked as though an admission had to be dragged from him. 'Yes, I knew her.'

Chris drew a deep breath. 'Well - when you disappeared, she was pregnant...with me.'

Gregson stared for a moment in silence. He had been gazing at Chris with a curious expression of reluctance, as though something he saw pained, even horrified him, but now he lowered his head into his hands. A sound came from him, like a deep sigh. Chris had rehearsed this scene many times in his thoughts, but never imagined its bleakness. Nothing was as he'd hoped it would be. He wanted to be somewhere else, not intruding on this private grief and bewilderment.

'What's your name?' Gregson said eventually, lifting his head and staring intently at his son's face.

'Chris.'

'Hello Chris.' He came across to shake hands, and clasped his son's shoulder. A hug between them, which Chris had often imagined, would have been all wrong. There had been too many hugs missing over the years. 'Forgive me,' Gregson said. 'I didn't know.'

'No.'

Chris was desperate not to do or say the wrong thing. He liked his father already. He liked his face, though it was marked by the care and disappointment of many years. He liked his voice, which was much like Chris's own. What he had not anticipated was the extent of his father's detachment from the world around him. He doubted whether Gregson could bring himself to 'like' his newly discovered son. As for love... The notion was something absurd, remote from the dark, half-life of the basement.

Nevertheless Gregson was struggling to make contact, from some state deeply withdrawn into himself. 'How is Susan?'

'She's OK.' Chris hardly knew how to handle that subject. 'She married.'

'I knew that,' his father said heavily. 'Is she happy?'

Chris shrugged in response to the impossible question. 'I don't know...'

'No.' The melancholy features creaked briefly into a smile. 'Sorry.' He moved towards the door. 'I was going to have some toast and Marmite when you rang. Do you like Marmite?'

'I love it.'

'So do I. Give me a moment and I'll get you some. Try and clear my head. I feel completely shell-shocked, tell you the truth.'

He drifted into the kitchen. It was obvious that he'd needed the breathing space, was unused to having people around him.

Chris felt pretty strange himself. Here they were together at last, father and son, and the whole world ignorant of it. He felt absurdly pleased that they shared a taste for Marmite.

After a while Gregson returned with the toast and they sat to eat it. 'How did you find me here?' he said.

'Sarah.'

His father nodded, but didn't ask after the woman he'd been married to for seven years, and not seen for more than ten.

'It's strange to find you sitting here,' Chris said, 'When there's a memorial stone to you at Potton Wood.'

Gregson looked blank. 'Potton Wood?'

'The place where your Lancaster crashed.'

'I didn't know.'

'You did crash there?' Chris asked, and got no reply. 'You *were* on the plane?' he persisted.

It seemed a great effort for his father to reply. 'Yes I was there,' he said eventually.

'Freddy said you'd have been on it.'

Gregson looked up at this. 'Freddy? Freddy Mitchell? You've seen him?'

'I've seen everyone.'

As had happened when Susan was mentioned, Freddy's name generated a brief spark of recognition. Gregson had rejected the past without escaping it. 'Is he all right?' he asked.

Chris decided on the truth. 'Not really.'

Gregson grunted but didn't follow that up either. There were similarities between the two former airmen, Chris thought. Not in their circumstances, but in mood: an absence of enthusiasm, a deadness.

They sat for a while without speaking, not uncomfortable, but not companionable either. Chris imagined the thousands of silent hours Gregson would have spent in the past decade. He tried to think of something that might engage his father's interest, and described the memorial ceremony at Cockayne Hatley.

'Not too many people get a memorial stone while they're still alive,' he said, trying for a glimmer of amusement from the situation.

'It suits me.' Gregson spoke in all seriousness. 'That's all over.' He was silent for another spell, and Chris had begun to think about leaving when his father spoke again. 'Would you like to hear what happened?'

'You mean the accident?'

'Yes, the accident.'

'I *would* like to know - I've thought so much about it. That is, if you don't mind telling me...'

Gregson started to talk in a slow, measured way, like a man giving a prepared speech at a conference. Probably this was only the second time he'd told the story, after Sarah. His eyes barely lifted from the ground. Chris imagined that the events were re-running through his father's mind in slow motion flashback, like something from an old black-and-white film.

~ Nineteen ~

18 September 1944

Gregson woke later than he intended on the morning after the mess party. When he raised his head from the pillow a wave of pain and dizziness surged through his temples. It took a moment for the pilot to identify it. The possessor of the famous 'iron head' had the distinctly unfamiliar experience of *a hangover*. The sight of Bitsa bounding about the room without a care in the world only made him feel grimmer. He skipped breakfast and stumbled about the quarters throwing his few personal effects into a bag. One of the last things to go in was the pewter tankard, a painful reminder of the previous evening's binge. Then, finally, the pilot's log books, the terse record of all his flights since he first went solo at the beginning of the war.

There were few goodbyes to say at the airfield before he took the transport to Bassingbourn, leaving without a backward glance. Pilots rarely became sentimental about individual bases, which were inhabited so intermittently and associated with fear and loss.

On reaching Bassingbourn Gregson located his quarters,

took some flying gear from his bag, and found an orderly to look after Bitsa. After taking orders from the station commander he went straight away to the mess. The plan was to lunch with the Australian crew detailed to receive instruction, then set off for a straightforward training flight lasting a couple of hours. Gregson could scarcely wait to get it over with. All he wanted to do was put his head down for a good night's sleep and recuperation.

He linked up first with the British engineer for the flight, a decent enough bloke, though Gregson couldn't help wishing that Freddy was still with him. The Aussies were introduced to them soon afterwards: the first pilot, engineer, navigator, and wireless operator. A second Australian pilot due to participate had been delayed by a bureaucratic mix-up, so that the crew would number six all told, rather than seven.

For Gregson lunch went by in something of a daze. Everything was unfamiliar: the location, the mess, the company, both English and Australian. The small talk was characteristic of two sets of strangers who were unlikely to see much more of each other. Gregson's head was pounding and he ate almost nothing. He was aware of falling down on his social duties, but getting through the day had to be the first priority. The Australians made little impression upon him, apart from the man he was sitting next to: the engineer, by name of Peter Freshwater. He was a stocky young chap, built upon Freddy lines and – like Freddy – seemed a mite more mature than the average airman. What is it about these engineers? Gregson thought to himself.

'I suppose you've done a lot of these training flights already?' Freshwater asked him.

'Tell you the truth, this is the very first one,' Gregson replied. 'I've been on operations. I finished my thirty trips two days ago, so I've come fresh to this job at Bassingbourn. Though to be honest...' - he paused to pass a hand wearily over his eyes – 'the word "fresh" doesn't exactly describe my condition at the moment.'

'No, you're looking a bit rough, mate.' Gregson was aware an unblinking gaze on him. The man had an extraordinarily broad, jowly face for one so young. 'All the same,' Freshwater said, 'Give me the man with experience every time. I'm glad you're taking us up.'

'Well thanks for that,' Gregson said lightly. 'Let's hope you live to repeat the compliment.'

After lunch they took the transport to their aircraft, and spilled out of it onto the grass areas around the aircraft's berth. It was the most delightful, balmy afternoon; the sun warmed their backs, and a light breeze freshened the atmosphere. Once out in the open, Gregson began to feel a lot better. The clean, country air filtered though his head, wafting out the debris from yesterday's over-indulgence. In a group they strolled across to where the aircraft was in the final stages of being prepared for flight. The Lancaster towered above them. No-one could have described that great bombing machine as beautiful, but Gregson nevertheless felt a rush of affection for it. He looked around him. The petrol bowser had just finished pumping high octane fuel into the plane's tanks and was pulling away to go back to base. The atmosphere for this training flight was so different to what he was used to on operations, when ground crews would often turn out in bulk to cheer their aircraft off. Here most of the ground staff had already dispersed and the sense of urgency was noticeably muted. Gregson resolved then and there that he would not allow the more relaxed environment to interfere with his pre-flight routines.

The Flight Sergeant in charge of the plane came up to him.

'Everything OK, Sergeant?' Gregson asked.

'She's fine, sir. We've given her a thorough going over. Engines are tip-top.'

'Good. Don't mind if I have a good look over her?'

'Of course, sir.'

'I'm sure you blokes already have your routines for take-off,' Gregson said, taking aside Freshwater and the first pilot, whose name was Turner. 'The ground staff on these bases are pretty good, I've found – I've every confidence in them, and I won't take off unless they assure me the craft's OK. At the same time I like to make certain myself.'

He walked round the Lancaster with the two Australians, checking the craft for leaks and looking at the tyre pressures.

Then he clambered up the outside of the fuselage as far as the cockpit, and called down to the ground staff Sergeant.

'Can you throw up that cloth, Sergeant.'

'Sir?'

'Don't mind me. It's a kind of ritual I've got into.'

The Sergeant looked on, a bit put out, as Gregson used the cloth religiously to polish the perspex cockpit screens.

'I always do it,' he said to the Aussies as he returned to earth. Visibility in these Lancaster cockpits is excellent, but it can't be good enough, especially at night.'

'All OK sir?' The Sergeant was still looking aggrieved.

'It's fine, Sergeant. We'll get the engines going, and I'll have a good listen to them, and then we can get away.' He signed the craft maintenance form.

'I'm afraid it's hello and goodbye for you and me, sir,' said the Sergeant. 'My last day at the base. I'm being transferred.'

'Then I hope things go well for you.'

A familiar barking sound made Gregson look up and see Bitsa thirty yards away, on a lead held by his orderly. The man was pulling back energetically to hold the dog in check. Some distance beyond that, on the edge of the airfield, something else caught his eye. A figure in uniform was cycling furiously round the perimeter, waving an arm in their direction. A shock of red hair flashed against the grassy background, so that Gregson was reminded of some bird of exotic plumage sweeping across a meadow.

'Who's this joker?' said Freshwater, with a pronounced Aussie tang in his voice.

Gregson sighed. 'His name's Patrick Stephens. I think he wants to go up with us.'

Stephens came hurtling up, leapt off the saddle like a rodeo rider, and hurried towards them.

'Just caught you, John,' he said a little breathlessly.

Gregson introduced him to the Australians.

'Remember what we were talking about?' said Stephens. 'I wondered if you had a spare place for me.'

'Well...we are a second pilot short. You've cleared it with the station commander, have you?'

Stephens looked evasive. 'Er...tell you the truth, John,

there hasn't been time. I only just made it up here.'

'Oh, I'm sorry Pat – I can't do it.'

Turner interrupted. 'This guy's a pilot, right?'

'He's a pilot all right,' Gregson said. 'One of the best.'

'If he's willing to help, I've no objections. Could come in useful.'

'Are you sure?' Gregson said doubtfully.

Stephens stood watching with the most winning of expressions plastered across his face; few could resist it.

'It's fine,' Turner said. 'We're not hung up on regulations over in Oz.'

Gregson glanced across at the Irishman. 'You're voted in, you jammy devil.'

'Hell, thanks you guys.' Stephens was grinning widely.

'Let's get going then.' Gregson turned away to board the Lancaster, but was almost knocked off his feet by a flying form which struck him around waist high. After this initial strike Bitsa, beside himself with agitation and excitement, began leaping high on the spot, pawing at the pilot's chest.

'Make a good kangaroo, this bugger,' Freshwater observed.

The orderly rushed forward to grab Bitsa's lead. 'I'm sorry, sir. He's a bit excitable. Pulled free of me.'

'That's OK,' said Gregson. 'It's just the new surroundings. He'll soon get used to them.' He bent to fondle the dog's ears. 'Go on, boy. Off with you. I'll be back soon.'

'Take him with us,' Stephens said suddenly, perhaps inspired by a surge of fellow-feeling for another outcast.

Gregson looked up. 'What a bad influence you are, Pat. Don't you know it's-'

'Against regulations? That old saw. Are you telling me he's never been up in a kite?'

Now it was Gregson's turn to look embarrassed. 'Well, he did once...'

'And how did he take to it? Stephens asked.

'Loved it.'

'Well then...'

Gregson hesitated. He wasn't a man for breaking rules. At the same time he felt a little concerned about the dog, which was naturally agitated on its first day at a new base. He glanced across at the Australians.

'Sure,' said Turner to the unspoken question, spreading his arms wide in mock exasperation. 'The more the merrier. Why don't we take waltzing Matilda along as well.'

With that they all clambered aboard and took up their station on the aircraft. The Australians had not flown Lancasters before and Gregson initially took the controls, with Turner beside him and the engineers and other crew behind. Bitsa curled up behind the pilot's seat. Gregson took Turner and the others through the procedures for checking the magnetos, oil pressure and temperature, and they also checked and set the gyro, cooling gills, and flaps. Eventually the crew reported ready.

Gregson pressed the start buttons and the engines coughed and roared as they fired. Columns of grey smoke and flame came from the exhaust. He sat still for a moment listening intently to the sound of the engines, and indicating some characteristic features to Turner and Freshwater. Then he throttled back to the tick-over positions and gave the thumbs-up sign to the ground staff, who pulled the chocks away from the aircraft's wheels: all procedures enacted hundreds of times before, in the same order, with the same results – the reassuring background to a successful take-off and flight. He pushed forward the throttles, to an answering roar from the engines, and trundled the Lancaster forward to its take-off position.

On a word from the control tower Gregson opened the throttles to maximum. The aircraft gathered speed, vibrating furiously and making its customary shattering row. He kept the nose down until the last minute, then lifted her clear. The Lancaster rose quickly, after a light kiss on the concrete runway. Turner took the wheels up, and she gathered speed. Gregson throttled back to climbing rpm to get to operating height, and gradually the engine noise changed to the familiar comforting hum. The aircraft was new to him, but he thought it seemed perfectly sound. The Australians had visibly relaxed as they saw that the English pilot knew his job.

The sky was virtually cloudless and the view through the perspex screens of the cockpit – personally polished by the pilot – made the very best of the flat English countryside. At their relatively low height of two thousand feet every house and tree stood out clearly. They passed an isolated farm house where a large table had been put out on the front lawn, spread with a white table-cloth. The image was so clear that Gregson thought he could distinguish the shapes of individual dishes on the surface.

The change, when it came, was sudden and dramatic. At one moment Gregson had a muted sense of well-being; the well-being that pilots experience during non-combat flights on sunny mornings. In the next he felt a reprise of the dizzy sickness that was far worse than his early morning hangover symptoms. As he gazed through the perspex, indicating something to Turner beside him, the sharp lines of the landscape started to turn fuzzy. A violent throbbing passed across his forehead and the turbulent sensation in his stomach returned, exacerbated by the close confines of the aircraft and the stench of fuel. He gagged in the cockpit.

'You OK?' asked Turner.

'I will be,' Gregson said, fighting off the nausea. 'Just feeling a bit under the weather.' He steadied himself, satisfied that he was fit to continue. 'OK – let's get on with the exercise. We're down to feather one of the engines today, so you can practise flying and landing on three. Ready to go?'

'Let's do it.'

'You take over then.'

Turner took over the controls and then cut the starboard outer engine. As he did so Gregson was struck by a second, more violent wave of nausea, and he involuntarily reached out to steady himself against Turner's shoulder. At the same time he ripped the intercom connection from his face, afraid that he was going to throw up into it. The moment passed and he replaced the equipment, but his head was swimming.

'Are you *sure* you're OK?' Turner said. 'You look awful.'

'I'm sorry about this,' Gregson said. 'I feel bad, I must admit. Not sure I can...'

Stephens's voice came on, interrupting him. 'Problems, John? If you're not feeling too hot, we can switch places for a while.'

'Go on,' Turner urged. 'You're in no condition.'

He made a decision. 'All right, Pat. Thanks. Let's do it. I'm glad you came along after all. I'll be OK in a while.'

They switched so that Turner and Stephens were in the pilot seats. Freshwater stood behind Stephens, whilst Gregson sat on the floor behind Turner, head down between his knees. The others were in the centre of the fuselage.

For a while Gregson was barely aware of events in the cockpit. He found he was just able to remain conscious with head down between his knees, but any attempt to rise brought immediate warning signals and the prospect of passing out. He sat there uncomfortable as hell, cursing his own irresponsibility – heavy drinking the night before and lack of sleep over the past two days. He had behaved in a way he would have condemned in any young pilot learning the trade, and it was no consolation to know that other colleagues had been just as feckless before him. He felt profoundly relieved that Stephens was, by a very fortunate chance, on board to take over.

Then he heard something which, even in his groggy condition, set off alarm bells. Every pilot became accustomed to the sound of the four engines which kept him in the air, and any alteration in their regular rhythm was a cause for concern. Because one engine had been feathered the Lancaster was flying on three. From his position on the floor Gregson now heard another engine splutter and cut out; the starboard inner, he was fairly sure. Instant confirmation came with Stephens's voice on the intercom.

'That's a bugger. We've lost an engine.'

Turner's voice came on. 'Shall I restart the outer?'

'As quick as you can. We're only at two thousand.'

Stephens's voice remained calm, but the situation was distinctly uncomfortable; two thousand feet was no height for a Lancaster with two engines out. Moments passed, but Gregson didn't catch the sound that was so urgently needed: that of a third engine getting back into action.

'She won't fire,' came a new voice, that of the British engineer.

'Try her again,' said Stephens, more urgently now.

'She won't fire,' said the man again.

Gregson felt a sudden lurch of fear. Out of nowhere a routine training flight was turning into an extremely serious situation, verging on the disastrous. There had been no warning. Acutely aware of his responsibility for the lives of all those in the aircraft he struggled to his knees, and was violently sick for his pains. He tore off the intercom, now in a disgusting state, and sank back with his head swimming.

Gregson thought he may have lost consciousness for a short while, for he had a dim sense of a break in the action. Yet when he raised his head to look around, nothing had changed. Stephens and Turner remained bent over the controls whilst Freshwater leant over the back of Stephens's seat, scrutinising the control dials for the source of the problem.

'Down to seven hundred feet,' came Freshwater's voice.

Gregson was mildly surprised to find he could still analyse the situation whilst on the verge of consciousness. With both starboard engines out, full left controls were needed merely to remain on a straight course. A right turn in these circumstances was suicidal and there was not enough central input available to bank or turn left. They would continue to go straight ahead, losing height steadily, until the aircraft hit the ground. Their only chance (and that rapidly diminishing) was to restart the feathered engine – the one that was unaccountably refusing to fire. He knew better than any of them how bleak were their chances now. The familiar atmosphere of the cockpit, with all its paraphernalia of equipment and indicators, encouraged a false sense of security, but of course it would provide no protection for an aircraft crash-landing at speed in open country.

Only the wireless operator – further back along the fuselage – would have been unaware of imminent disaster, but there was no sense of panic in the craft. Very little was said, though Gregson saw Turner and Freshwater exchange a glance which, more than anything, conveyed the seriousness of their situation. Stephens continued patiently to search for a solution, as Gregson would have expected of him. It was odd, he thought, that men could go to their deaths in this stolid, uncomplaining way. He could scarcely believe it was happening himself, after all his thousands of flying hours, most of them over enemy territory. Despite the continuing racket of two engines it seemed unnaturally quiet in the cockpit, as if all the usual circumstances of flight were in suspension.

Briefly, Gregson considered trying to stumble to his feet to help, but he was sentient enough to know that this would only make things worse. Better to leave things in the capable hands of Pat Stephens. He stayed where he was, with the warm shape of Bitsa pressed up against his side; the dog was sleeping, oblivious to the anxieties of the men all around. From the corner of his eye Gregson saw Freshwater crouch down behind the pilot's seat. With a start of memory he put a hand to his left arm, and felt Sarah's garter underneath his uniform. He had put it there in his room, on impulse. After the past couple of days it had seemed all wrong to take along Susan's nylon stocking, though it had brought him and the crew safely through so many dangerous flights. It was absurd, of course; but also difficult now not to see it as an ill omen.

Suddenly Gregson wanted very much to see the place where he was likely to die. He took a deep breath and heaved himself up so that his head was level with the perspex screens of the cockpit. The Lancaster was a mere couple of hundred feet up, above ground which was rising gently ahead of them. Less than a mile ahead he could make out the dark mass of a small wood. Turning his head he saw, a hundred yards from the trees, an elegant grey-stone church with a square tower, surrounded by grass verges and greenery, and white grave-stones showing palely in the sunlight.

***   ***   ***

Gregson woke with the memory of a nightmare so intense that for a long minute he confused dream and reality. The Lancaster had been involved in an accident. On hitting the ground it had caught fire, every airman's dread. He was trapped in the cockpit and could feel the flames at his face. He panicked and tried to pull clear but his feet were trapped somewhere and scarcely moved.

He opened his eyes and saw leaves and bracken on the surface of the earth. Bitsa was beside him, licking at his face with a quiet, steady rhythm. For a moment his doggy scent dominated everything. Gregson reached out a hand and fondled the dog's ear, a familiar movement in a strange landscape.

'All right, Bitsa. Thanks.'

He rolled over and sat up with great difficulty. His head ached and there was an area of intense pain at the back of his neck, as though someone had struck there with a heavy sandbag. Something was wrong with his right arm, too; the sleeve was discoloured and underneath it blood had congealed on a long cut.

He wasn't thinking straight, he knew that; all the same there ought to be a plane nearby, or at worst the remains of one. Instead he was in a small clearing in a wood, apparently alone. There was no sign of wreckage. A heavy mist lay over the landscape making everything indistinct. All he could see were tree trunks, and more tree trunks beyond them. The scene was remarkably still.

Beyond the pain of his injuries, which seemed relatively minor, considering what must have happened, Gregson felt a severe sense of disorientation. To find himself alone like this in a forest clearing was beyond comprehension. Where was the aircraft? Where his fellow fliers? Why had helpers not arrived to find survivors, when the plane's descent would have been clearly visible in the surrounding countryside? Perhaps the head injury had disturbed his capacity for logical thought. Certainly he felt very strange, as though this were an out-of-body experience and nothing was as it seemed.

Bitsa was gazing at his master with a dog's air of expectancy and it was this, rather than any personal desire to move, that got Gregson levered onto his knees and thence, hesitatingly, up to the vertical. He felt unsteady, but no bones had been broken and walking seemed an option. But where to? There was no landmark in sight and the sun was obscured by mist. This was the navigator's nightmare, being adrift in a strange landscape without a compass. What would Freddy have done? 'Instinct, my boy – it's the one thing they can't teach you at flying school.' Well now was the time to test his own instinct. He started walking, head down, watching with a curious detachment his own feet move across the grass and bracken of the forest floor.

Gregson continued in this way for some time until he came across a mud path and, still trusting to instinct, turned right along it. He trudged on, feeling strength returning to his body, though to compensate for this his head began to ache even more ferociously. Bitsa charged ahead, turning at intervals to ensure that his master remained in sight. The going was easier now, but still no sign of human habitation appeared. And then from nowhere a line of telegraph poles sprang up out of the forest, and Gregson found himself standing beside a narrow tarmac road that ran between the trees.

This time there was no need to decide on a direction. No sooner had he stepped onto the tarmac than the sound of a vehicle broke the silence, and within seconds a small white van could be seen coasting down the country lane. Gregson instinctively raised a hand and the van stopped beside him. They always stop for uniforms, he thought.

The driver poked his head out of the side window, clearly surprised to find an airman and a dog in the remote location.

'What's happened to you, son?'

'Accident.'

'What sort of accident?'

'Oh...nothing much.'

At this moment Gregson would have said that he had no thought about the future. Putting one foot in front of the other was as much as he could manage. Yet already he found himself prevaricating. He didn't know it, but this was the moment when his whole life took a new and unconsidered turning.

'Where are you headed?' asked the van driver.

'Anywhere would be better than this,' Gregson said. 'I want to get to Cambridge.' The words came without hesitation. He could have said 'Bassingbourn', but didn't.

'I'm going to Cambridge,' the driver said.

'Do you think you could take me – and my dog here?'

'Hop in.'

He got the door open and clambered onto the front seat, encouraging Bitsa to leap up beside him. When he tried to slide the door back to the closed position his limbs refused to react, and the driver had to lean across him to finish the job. The man was middle-aged, with a comfortable paunch covered by fawn overalls. As the vehicle moved off he gave his passenger a searching look.

'Are you sure you're all right, son?'

Gregson propped himself against a window and rested his head on one hand. The confined atmosphere of the van reminded him too closely of the Lancaster's cockpit.

'I'll be OK. Got a bang on the head.' He found himself wanting to change the subject, and sniffed the air. 'Smells nice in here. What is it?'

'Can't you tell?' The driver was looking at him askance.

'Don't know.' He couldn't place it; everything was confused.

'Bread, of course,' the man explained, as if to a child. 'I supply products from the bakery.'

They went on in near silence, at first through countryside that was unfamiliar to Gregson, then past some recognisable landmarks in the outskirts of Cambridge.

'Whereabouts in Cambridge?' the driver said.

Gregson blinked. 'Anywhere will do.'

'Oh no.' The man was still giving his passenger a searching gaze. 'And have your wandering about in a daze. Tell me where you live, son. I'll take you there.'

The airman stared at him for a moment, then heard his voice giving Sarah's address. Though he'd only been there once, the details were clear in his mind.

'Right you are then.'

Ten minutes later Gregson was knocking at the door of Sarah's lodgings. In the street the bread van drove away with its driver giving a cheerful thumbs-up gesture through the window. The suburban street was quiet – deserted, even – and at first there was no response from the house. The pilot waited, hoping against hope for some sign of life from within. And if there was none? Could he turn away now, try to make his way back to the airfield? More likely, sit in the gutter with head in his hands.

The door opened and a plump face looked out, a face spread with too much make-up. He'd been thinking of Sarah, but it was her landlady who answered the door.

'Are you all right, love?' she said. Everyone was asking this.

'I think so.' Gregson wasn't sure. 'I'm a friend of Sarah's.'

'Of course.' He saw recognition dawn through the make-up. 'Sorry, dear. I thought your face was familiar.'

'Is she here?'

'Hold on a tic.'

The woman went away, leaving Gregson on the door-step. The throbbing in his head had almost eliminated thought, but suddenly – absurdly – he remembered Sarah's garter, and reached down to touch the thing. At least it had got him through the crash, he thought. At least he'd survived.

A sound from the doorway made him look up, and Sarah stood in front of him.

'John!'

He knew from her face that she'd never expected to see him again. Yet she was overjoyed to find him there now; that much was also clear. And she had a different expression that he found impossible to interpret.

'Sarah. You did say if I...do you think I could come in for a bit?'

She stepped down and put her arms round him, her face against his. Her unmistakable body scent floated into his nostrils. Her strength seemed to pass into him.

'It's lovely to see you,' she said. 'Come on up.'

~ Twenty ~

October 1964

Gregson lifted his head and gazed at his son like a man coming out of hypnotism. 'So that's what happened,' he said. 'All that I'm aware of, anyway. How much of it did you know?'

Chris shook his head. 'I didn't *know* any of it, of course. I talked to Freddy and he thought Stephens must have been on the flight. I went across to Belfast and talked to his sister.

She knew he was dead all along.'

Gregson looked down at the rug. 'I should have let the family know. There was no excuse.'

'If you had, your story would have come out.'

'Too bad.'

Nothing Chris might say would have smoothed over the uncomfortable truth about Stephens, and he changed the subject. 'Freddy guessed Bitsa was on board, too. He said dogs were great survivors.'

'I've no idea how Bitsa and I got out,' Gregson said. 'You seem to be very well informed. Perhaps you can tell me.'

'Do you know what happened to the plane?'

'I don't know anything. In a show like that you don't want to know.'

Gregson was almost crouching in his chair, arms held protectively across his body. Chris remembered what Freshwater had said in the church: that it had taken him twenty years to come to terms with the crash.

'What they told me is that one wing of the Lancaster hit the trees,' Chris said, 'It slewed round and ploughed into the wood.'

'That's it then. The body of the plane must have split open at that point. I was against the fuselage and out I went, Bitsa with me. Thrown clear. The Lanc would have skidded on for quite a bit. Burst into flames, I suppose?'

'The fire destroyed everything.'

'You can see how lucky I was.' Gregson's tone suggested he wasn't too sure about that. 'I couldn't see the aircraft when I came to, and to be honest I don't think I looked. I must have been in a strange sort of way.'

'All the same it's surprising the local people didn't find you when they got the other bodies out,' Chris said.

'They wouldn't have known I was there, would they?' Gregson said slowly. 'Because of Stephens. His body. It's odd they didn't hear Bitsa though. Normally he'd have barked.' He sighed, almost groaned. 'I really don't know what happened.'

With an effort, Chris restrained himself from firing off more questions. It was clear that speech - the mere act of communication - was an enormous effort for his father. He was only attempting it at all from a sense of guilt; to atone for past sins, as he saw them. They sat together in silence in the darkened basement room. A car went past in the road outside, and the headlights briefly registered on Gregson's wall. This was where his father had shut himself away for the past 20 years, Chris thought; it was as though he were buried alive.

'What else would you like to know?' Gregson had gathered himself to make another effort.

'There's something I don't quite understand...' Chris sought the words for another difficult enquiry. 'You didn't go back to your base.'

Gregson avoided his eyes. 'It's hard to understand now. I just wanted to get my head down.'

'But the people at the airfield. Didn't they come looking for you?'

'Before long I realised - they thought I was dead. I *meant* to go back there, but...I never did. I spent a couple of days with Sarah. She stayed on at the guest house to look after me. Then I stayed a bit longer...and longer. She made enquiries and found out I was supposed to be dead, and bit by bit I thought - why not stay out of it. It sounds odd, I know, but I just didn't go back. I'd had enough. All sorts of reasons. I'm not trying to make excuses but for a while it seemed wonderful, not having to return.'

I can understand that,' Chris said, and he meant it. 'And they never found you.'

'Hard to believe, isn't it, but yes. I got away with it. I don't think they even looked. I didn't realise at the time but there was the confusion over Stephens...well, I'd have realised if I wanted to, but I didn't.'

'No.'

'Of course there were thousands of deserters in Britain after the war, but it was easier for me. I was supposed to have been killed. Sarah and I went up to the Lake District, right away from it all - with Bitsa, of course. All the same...' he said bitterly. 'It was all wrong. For years, you couldn't hold your head up. Deserters were shamed. Many of them took to crime. There were all sorts of practical difficulties, with ration cards and so on. You had to create a new identity. And you needed some luck.' Gregson's brooding face showed his misery all too clearly. 'I'm not excusing myself. It was wrong.'

'You'd done enough,' Chris broke out. 'So much more than most people. You'd no need to feel bad about it.'

'Thank you,' Gregson said, giving his son a sad smile. 'I've needed someone to tell me that over the past ten years, when I was running this stuff over and over in my mind. I was wrong all the same. I lost my self-respect. To be fair to her, Sarah backed me up. She had a hard time of it, one way and another.'

It was the first time he'd spoken of Sarah. Chris began to say something about her, but Gregson stopped him.

'No excuses there either. I've been involved with two women in my life and spoilt things for both of them.'

This was the opening Chris wanted. 'Yes, I need to talk about my mother. I want to tell her about you.'

'No,' Gregson said, speaking more forcefully than he had up to now. 'No, don't do that. I beg you not to.'

'I'm sure she would want to know.'

'It can only do harm. You already said it - she's married.'

'Yes, she married soon after I was born. A widower – Reg - with two children.'

'I heard about it. That kept me away. It cost me a lot at the time, and I don't want to spoil it for her now.' For almost the first time he looked Chris properly in the eyes. 'I didn't hear about you, though. That might have changed matters.'

Chris felt a little shaft of hope in the gloom of the basement room. 'Well you do know about me now,' he said. 'Contact my mother, will you, please?.'

'Don't stir things up, I beg you.'

'You can't leave her in the dark any more. Suppose she wants to meet you. Would you see her?'

'Don't do it,' Gregson said, with finality.

When he'd first knocked on the door Chris felt he could have stayed in his father's company for days, for years if need be. Yet already he sensed the strain of the situation, one that was so unnatural to both of them. Part of him wanted already to leave this airless room, to walk in the street outside and breathe in air from the living world. He liked the man who sat opposite and felt sorry for him, but the closeness he'd hoped for between father and son hadn't happened (beyond a shared liking for Marmite). How could it have done? They *had* no shared experience; nothing to discuss beyond the strangeness of the situation. Not even the age-old aggravations between the generations. And if the meeting had been a strain for him, he thought, how much more so for his father?

So Chris said he had to leave. They talked a little bit longer about some mundane matters before Gregson saw him to the door. Rain had begun to fall and the basement well outside was awash. Neither of them had mentioned a future meeting.

'By the way,' Chris said, outside the front door. 'You passed on your obsession with aircraft. I've a three-foot bomber in my bedroom. Been modelling it for months.'

'A Lancaster, I hope,' Gregson said, unsmiling.

Chris, up the basement steps by now, paused in the street above. 'No, a Liberator,' he called down.

His father shouted back up to him. 'Oh no - you've got that wrong. The Lanc was *the* bomber in the war. You couldn't beat them.'

***   ***   ***

It was late when Chris reached home, and the house was in darkness. No-one stirred when he let himself in and quietly ascended the stairs. He'd half-hoped Alison might come out to ask about his trip, but she was obviously asleep. Another part of him was glad to keep her out of it. In the recent past he'd leaned heavily upon his 'sister' for advice but there was one question that he must now resolve on his own. A question that kept him awake through the night, thrashing about in bed, eventually rising in the small hours to sit head in hands at his desk. What should he tell his mother?

And yet he knew, at some level of consciousness, that he was going to tell her Gregson was alive. It was less a decision than a recognition of what had be done. He gave little weight to the pain this would cause Reg, but – and he was later to reflect that this was a step forward – he did know it would cause pain. He even realised that he had never taken Reg's feelings sufficiently into account. Pain caused to his mother was a different matter. But he knew himself what it was like to be kept in the dark about something of the utmost importance, and he wouldn't inflict that on her. He would tell her, and do it as soon as possible.

The opportunity soon came. When he went down for breakfast Reg had left for work and his mother was alone in the kitchen.

'The wanderer returns,' she said. 'You look terrible. As if you haven't had a wink of sleep.'

'I haven't,' he said, feeling the moment rushing upon him and submitting to it helplessly.

'What is it?' she said, with a darkening face.

'Why don't you sit down, Mum.'

'What is it? she repeated.

Sitting at the kitchen table he gestured towards the chair opposite, and she sat down without taking her eyes from him. He was reminded of Mary Stephens sitting across from him in her own kitchen, and this gave him a way in.

'You know I've been looking into my father's accident,' he said. His mother made no response. 'Talking to Freddy,' he went on, 'And to the local man who helped at the crash, I started to realise there was another airman on that plane. Someone who shouldn't have been there. A pilot, called Patrick Stephens. Did you ever meet him?'

She shook her head.

'Red-haired?'

Still she sat silent.

'Well anyway, I was right about that. I've just been to see Stephens's sister in Belfast. He disappeared at the time of the accident. He was on the aircraft.'

And now Chris wished he hadn't started. He had never seen such an expression on his mother's face: feverish, almost haunted. He felt like a man about to break the worst possible news, rather than something good. Or was it good? He had no idea.

'There should have been six men on the plane, and they

found six bodies all right...but one of them was Stephens's.'
He plunged on remorselessly. 'Everyone thought it was my
father's, but it was Stephens.' He reached out to cover his
mother's hand with his own. 'My father's alive,' he said. 'I
saw him last night. He's alive.'

If there was a moment when he regretted the long pursuit of
the truth it was then; regretted buying a car and asking for his
driving licence, getting in touch with his father's aunt, all that
followed it. His mother sat staring ahead. She was
somewhere else, two decades away. It seemed scarcely
possible that anyone could remain so still. Then a single tear
ran down her face and she raised a hand to wipe it away.

'All this time,' she said.

'Yes. All this time.'

She still sat silently, but her face was calmer now. Close as
they were, Chris found it impossible to divine her thoughts.
The past was another world: hardship, excitement, air raid
warnings, waggling wings, uniforms, all neatly tidied away.
How could she bridge those times and the sedate, semi-
detached existence of the 1960s? A person only had one life
to live.

She lifted her head and spoke in a tone that was almost
normal. 'How is he?' she said.

~ Twenty one ~

October 1964

Once the ice had been broken it was easy to proceed. Chris
told his mother everything he knew. He told her Gregson had
married Sarah and separated years ago; that he was alone,
withdrawn and unhappy; that he'd begged his son not to tell
Susan, but also that he'd asked after her. Everything.

His mother made little comment at the time, but the next
day she came into Chris's room and said 'I want to see him'.
That was how she put it, and Chris didn't have to ask who
'him' was. She asked if Chris would be the go-between in
setting up a meeting. She'd told Reg about it; he wasn't very

happy - in fact, had tried to stop her - but in the end conceded that she needed this chance to meet the father of her first child. Chris was astonished by the composed way his mother took this decision, and by the speed of it.

He did his bit as the go-between and fixed the meeting. Surprisingly, Gregson agreed to it without demur. Perhaps he'd wanted to see Susan all along but made his last-ditch attempt to avoid tangling her life. Perhaps he was passive in this as in all aspects of his current existence, and yielded to anyone who pushed hard enough. Whatever the reason they arranged that Chris would drive his mother to Islington one morning; she would spend some time with Gregson, then find her own way back.

The day for their reunion arrived. Reg went to work as usual and Susan got herself ready to leave. At breakfast she'd not struck Chris as being particularly nervous, but her actions had been unusually brisk. When she came to his room to say 'Ready!' she was wearing a dark skirt and white blouse combination; it gave her an institutional appearance, as though she were a hotel receptionist or conference facilitator.

He pulled a face. 'Can't you wear one of your nice dresses - something a bit more frivolous?'

'And here's the great expert on women's clothing,' she said.

All the same she went away and came back ten minutes later in a dress that was less formal. Some jazzy earrings had appeared too.

'That's more like it,' he said.

Actually, he thought she looked wonderful.

'Are you prepared to drive me now?' she said.

'I'm at your service, madam.'

They talked little as he took Clara across London. The day was overcast and humid, and as he reached Islington the sky opened. Chris pulled up outside his father's door and they sat in the car for a minute while rain poured down the windscreen. He looked across at the passenger seat. His mother's eyes were glittering. She wore no make-up yet her face was highly coloured. She was the same person, but oddly different; a lot younger, for one thing.

'Wish me luck,' she said.

'You're not going to need it.'

She leaned across and kissed him, then jumped out and ran down the steps to Gregson's basement. In the rain she looked like a carefree girl. Chris had a strange presentiment: that she was running away from him towards someone who mattered more. It was something he'd never felt when she was with Reg. He felt glad now that he'd told her. He waited in the car until his father's door opened, then drove away.

Back home the day passed with excruciating slowness. Because the arrangement was open-ended Chris had no idea when she'd be back. He prowled the house, unable to settle; played a few records on his turntable; sat down and for the first time in weeks started some work on the Liberator model, but his heart wasn't in it.

He longed to know what was happening in that Islington basement. He'd no real expectations of the meeting, but he wanted them to hit it off, to be free of bitterness. Time was too short for more unhappiness. Perhaps they might see each other from time to time, if Reg could be reconciled to it. Chris played a few records on his turntable. He sat down and for the first time in weeks started some work on the Liberator model, but his heart wasn't in it.

Reg came in at five-thirty, earlier than usual, and Alison and Gary followed soon after. They all snatched meals individually rather than eating together. When it reached eight o'clock and Susan hadn't returned Chris began to feel concerned. She'd been away for ten hours, long surpassing her expected absence. Reg clearly found the delay intolerable. He paced up and down the hallway with a haunted expression. After nine he went out into the dark garden and hacked at an old tree stump with an axe, unprecedented behaviour.

Chris heard her come in well after ten. He hoped his mother would come and report how things had gone but instead she went straight into her bedroom with Reg. He heard the murmur of their voices. Half an hour later she knocked on Chris's door, and stood just inside, breathing quite heavily. Her eyes looked feverish.

'How did it go?' Chris almost shouted in his anxiety.

She ignored this. 'We've always been close, haven't we,

you and me?' she said. 'Sometimes I used to think, almost too close. There were reasons for it.'

'Mum...?' If he hadn't known better, he'd have thought his mother was on drugs, she was on such a high.

'You've changed in the last few months,' she went on, sweeping aside his interruption. 'All this business about John, what you've done...it's changed you. I like what I've seen.' She laughed frenetically. 'Oh, the proud mother - so embarrassing for her son.'

She took a step forward, put her arms out, and held him. 'Be happy for me, Chris.'

'Always,' he said, wondering where this was going. Her self-assurance was so uncharacteristic. He began to speak but she interrupted again.

'I have to go.' Now she was speaking almost formally. 'Would you go down to the living room for a moment? There's something I want to say, to the three of you. Best to do it with all of us together.'

He went down and was soon joined by Gary and Alison. Reg was nowhere to be seen. They waited for Susan to appear, like a group of wartime pilots awaiting their briefing officer.

She came in looking very pale, clutching a handkerchief in one hand and a suitcase in the other. She spoke in voice which wobbled but never tipped over into crying. 'I'm sorry about this silly scene,' she said. 'I couldn't think of another way of doing it. I've loved all three of you always, so I thought - talk to you all together. I hope that's the best way. It's a sort of announcement. You know about John - Chris's father. I was close to him 20 years ago and then...I thought he was dead. I've been to meet him today. When we saw each other again I found nothing had changed. I felt the way I did about him before, when we messed things up between us.' She dabbed at her eyes with the handkerchief but continued. Chris was amazed at her resilience. 'I felt like a young woman again,' she said, with an embarrassed little laugh. 'He feels something for me too. I don't know how this will go but we have to give it a try. He's waiting outside in his car. I'm going to go there tonight and live with him.'

The three members of her audience all gasped audibly and Alison raised a hand to her mouth, but Susan plunged on.

'I'm not worried about you three. You're all grown up and can look after yourselves. You already do. I hope you'll come and see me as often as you like. I'm not far away. I've told Reg about my decision. I feel guilty and miserable about leaving here, after all he's done for me...' Susan had no need to say it, for guilt was inscribed on her face. She gathered herself with determination and went on. 'This is my decision. John didn't want me to break up my home. I had to persuade him. I've spent all day doing it. I know it's right. He needs me and...well, I love him,' she said simply. 'I'm sorry.'

She turned to leave but Alison, with her instinct for the right gesture, crossed the room and hugged her. They held each other for a moment. Chris went over and took her hand. Even Gary looked upset and suspiciously near to tears.

After the event Chris was astonished by the speed of her departure. Within five minutes of announcing the news she had gone. The three of them gathered in the front garden as she went to the gate, suitcase in hand. There was a faint absurdity about the reversal of customary roles, the offspring watching their parent leave the family home. An unfamiliar car was parked at the kerb. When she reached it, Gregson got out to open the passenger door and helped her inside. Chris took a step towards his father then stopped himself. It was not his moment.

Back in the house an air of shock lingered in the rooms and on the stairway. As the instigator of this chain of events Chris found his own thoughts were in confusion. In seeking a father he'd not anticipated losing a mother but it had happened. Despite the pain it had caused he was happy for her sake. He would see his mother often enough but she'd be with someone she loved. That was how it should be. In time, perhaps, his father would get used to the idea of a son. And Chris could become a son, however late in the day.

He now became acutely aware of the person who'd lost out during these events. When Alison went upstairs he knew she'd gone to talk to Reg, who had not left his room since Susan's departure. For the first time in his life Chris thought how his surrogate father must be feeling. He knew Reg would hold him responsible for what had happened, and with good reason. He saw blame in Alison's eyes too when they passed each other silently in the hall.

Chris was in the lounge around midnight when a loud crash came from above. He went up the stairs two at a time. Alison was standing on the landing, and gestured towards Chris's bedroom.

Inside, Reg was sitting on the bed, head in arms. His body seemed smaller than usual, its power and energy dissipated. The stand holding the Liberator was overturned and the model lay on the floor broken into several pieces. The fuselage had been smashed in.

Chris sat on the bed beside Reg and put a hand on his shoulder, a gesture that was less strange than he had anticipated.

'I'm sorry,' Chris said. A word trembled on his lips. 'I'm sorry...Dad.'

Reg in turn reached awkwardly up to put a hand on Chris's arm, so that they sat conjoined in an unnatural posture, like two chimpanzees. Eventually he lifted his head. 'It's not your fault, Chris,' he said in an unrecognisable voice. 'It was me. I drove her away.'

'It wasn't like that.' Chris sat quite still, wanting to help. 'Can I do anything for you?'

'You just have,' Reg said.

'Come down and have a cup of tea.'

'All right.'

They went down and sat together at the kitchen table, an act which again seemed less unnatural than he'd have imagined two days earlier.

A little later Alison knocked and came into Chris's room. She'd been crying. The urge to acknowledge blame, which had afflicted the whole household, came over him again. He began to apologise but she reached up and put a finger to his lips.

'No-one must be sorry,' she said. 'It just happened. They should have been together 20 years ago. Dad's feeling a bit better now, thanks to you. I think he knew it was going to happen.' She took a step forward so that they were very close. 'All this emotion in one day. You know what? I feel like cashing in on the mood. Taking a really big risk.'

'What do you mean?'

'Everything changed when we discovered who your father was.' She reached out to touch him. 'You do realise we don't have to behave like brother and sister now.'

He knew instantly what she meant, but couldn't help recoiling. 'It would seem so strange...'

'We could get over that.' As always, she was stronger and more certain than him. 'It just needs a mental leap.'

'I've always felt close to you...'

'How did Susan put it?' she interrupted. '"You'll know when it's the one." She and your father knew 20 years ago, but the story took a wrong turning. It was like *Wuthering Heights*.'

'What's that?'

'It's a book, you ignorant berk.' She punched his arm playfully. 'You *know* we're soul-mates. You just need to admit it to yourself. I'll give you some time to adjust.'

'Oh yes. Like what?'

'A week.'

He grinned. 'And then what?'

She gazed up at him, and already she looked different. 'I'll expect you to screw the living daylights out of me.'

~ Twenty two ~

October 1964

Susan's departure to Islington was almost the end of the story. A few loose ends remained, from the bizarre situation of a man dying yet being found alive, and most of them were destined to stay loose. Chris rang the number Peter Freshwater had given him and caught the Australian just before his return home. Freshwater heard through Chris's account of what had happened. 'Congrats,' he said at length. 'S'pose you're feeling pretty chipper?'

'Actually it takes some getting used to,' Chris said. 'I'm glad for my mother. She's a different person already.' He was sorry they were on the phone, as there was a rather tricky matter to raise. 'I wanted to ask you a favour concerning my father,' he said.

'I think I can guess. You mean the discrepancy in the accident report. You want me to keep mum. Seven equals six.'

'Something like that.' Chris was embarrassed at finding the Australian ahead of him. 'I don't know what would happen if the authorities knew the full story. He could find himself in trouble.'

'I doubt it after 20 years,' Freshwater said. 'What about the ginger-haired character? He must have relatives somewhere.'

'He has a sister. I've been to see her. She'll leave it be.'

There was a brief silence on the other end of the line. 'All right, Chris, you've got it. Discrepancy - what discrepancy? Last thing you want is those official guys poking over the entrails.'

'Thank you,' Chris said, and he meant it. 'Thank you very much.'

'It's OK. And don't forget to come and see me in Sydney one day.'

Chris had another call to make. When he told Freddy Mitchell his father was alive Freddy's reactions ranged from disbelief to indignation that Gregson had not contacted him, and finally to acceptance.

'Just give him my address,' he said.

'I will, but it could be a while before he gets in touch. He's kind of passive. A loner.'

'A few years with your mother will change that. When he wants to contact me he will. You know, maybe your Dad made the right choice dealing with those war years, shutting them out. You can hardly say my way's been a success, can you. Good luck, Chris.'

Did he need luck, Chris wondered. He'd started college now, and a new way of life. Looking into his father's accident had taught him an awful lot about the way people behaved, what was important and what wasn't; not least, the way he behaved himself. He'd put away some of his childish things.

(There would be no more modelling of aircraft, for a start.) He'd been cut free from his mother's apron strings, not before time, and found a father; and if he and Reg both worked at it, maybe two fathers. And he seemed to have lost a sister and found a girl he loved. All because he'd needed a birth certificate for his driving licence.

There was one other thing he had to do before the Lancaster could be definitively buried in Potton Wood. He phoned Derry Holmes with an enquiry.

'As it happens I think there *is* room on the stone,' Derry said, 'Though it's pure luck. It'll be a bit tricky technically. Can't really pull the thing out again. I'll have to carve it in place. If we get some good weather I should be able to do it in half a day, there in the churchyard - as long as the vicar will let me.'

'I'll talk to David Threlfall,' Chris said. 'And I'll recompense you for your trouble, of course.'

'Oh no,' Derry said. 'I shan't be charging you for that.'

It was mid-October before Derry found a suitable day and went up to Cockayne Hatley to do the work. And later still - at the end of the month - before Chris drove up to Liverpool to collect Mary Stephens from the Belfast ferry, before travelling South again to Bedfordshire. That was a long drive for Clara but she behaved well. Maybe she felt a little responsible, after setting the whole thing in motion.

David Threlfall met them at the church, having insisted on conducting a short blessing ceremony for the addition to the stone. He apologised to Mary for being a priest from the wrong denomination and she smiled and said she wasn't bothered by that kind of thing. She knelt by the stone and ran her fingers over the name of Patrick Stephens, inscribed in the list of men killed. Threlfall read a prayer and a blessing as the three of them stood by the memorial facing Potton Wood. Winter was close at hand, and leaves scurried across the open ground. Mary stood with head bowed, wiping away her tears with a gloved hand.

If there was anyone who could understand how she felt it was Chris himself. He'd stood there a mere six weeks earlier with the same sense of ancient loss. He looked down at the stone and the name of 'J Gregson' inscribed there. He'd not told Mary that his father was alive, nor Threlfall or Derry for that matter. Let the name remain on the slate. Flight Lieutenant John Gregson had ended his life in 1944. As Threlfall completed the blessing Chris found himself praying. He prayed that a new man would emerge from the shell of the old one.

~ The end ~

Historical note

The characters in this novel are fictional, but the plot is loosely linked to a real event. My own father, a pilot, was killed in an aircraft accident as he trained Australian airmen towards the end of the war. The accident occurred near Cockayne Hatley in Bedfordshire. My mother was not aware that anyone had survived, and the details remained unknown at the time. Decades later my brother investigated the incident and made contact with the three survivors – two Australians and one Englishman.

My brother organised a memorial service at the Cockayne Hatley church, which was quite similar to the one depicted in the novel. There was even an appearance from a Spitfire, laid on by the vicar. And the Cockayne Hatley churchyard now contains a memorial stone listing the names of all the airmen who took part in the ill-fated flight. (A dog called 'Bitsa' is listed too, but it died in the crash.) The churchyard also contains the gravestone of the little girl who knew J M Barrie.

All the other details in the novel – the characters and the relationships between them, and the appearance of a 'seventh man' – were invented by me.

If you enjoyed this book, please do add 'Pilot Error' to your liked pages on Facebook.

Printed in Great Britain
by Amazon